THE ERIE CANAL

RALPH K. ANDRIST

AMERICAN HERITAGE • NEW WORD CITY

Published by New Word City LLC, 2016
www.NewWordCity.com

American Heritage Publishing
Edwin S. Grosvenor, President
P.O. Box 1488
Rockville, MD 20851

For more information about American Heritage, visit our website at
www.AmericanHeritage.com.

1

A NEW WAY WEST

During the summer of 1777, the American revolutionary army was retreating down the Hudson River from General John Burgoyne's British redcoats and hired Hessians. Fort Ticonderoga had been outflanked and abandoned without a shot being fired; the chances that the new American nation would last much longer looked very gloomy.

It hardly seemed a time to be talking about great plans for the future, especially something as vast as a canal to span the wilderness of upper New York. But that was exactly what Gouverneur Morris, a member of the First Continental Congress, chose to discuss one night during the retreat. Morris had traveled to Fort Edward, north of Troy, to see how things were going with the ragged army. And one evening, as mist settled over the northern forest and the air grew chill, he sat in a warm farmhouse kitchen with a group of officers and spoke of the future of the country.

Morgan Lewis - one of the officers in the demoralized camp and later a New York state senator and governor - remembered Morris as brimming with optimism "even in the most gloomy periods of the war." He never doubted, Lewis said, "the ultimate triumph of our arms and the consequent attainment of our independence," and "frequently amused us by descanting with great energy on what he termed 'the rising glories of the western world.'"

South of where they stood, the Mohawk River joined the Hudson from the west. Morris painted a word-picture of a peaceful waterway which would extend from the Hudson, through the valley of the Mohawk, all the way to Lake Erie. He spoke, according to Officer Lewis, of the day "when the waters of the great western inland seas would, by the aid of man, break through their barriers and mingle with those of the Hudson." These waters, Morris said, would carry an endless procession of boats bearing passengers and goods to and from the western territories of the new country by way of the Great Lakes. Asked how it could be done, Morris answered that "numerous streams passed through natural channels, and that artificial ones might be conducted by the same routes," recalled Morgan Lewis.

Later, Morris wrote an exuberantly prophetic letter about such a waterway in which he said, "As yet, we only crawl along the outer shell of our country. The interior excels the part we inhabit in soil, in climate, in everything. The proudest empire in Europe is but a bubble compared to what America *will* be, *must* be, in the course of two centuries, perhaps of one." He quipped to a friend: "Shall I lead your astonishment to the verge of incredulity? I will: know then, that one-tenth of the expense born by the British in the last campaign would enable ships to sail from London through Hudson's river into Lake Erie."

Morris was one of the first to seriously consider the tremendous potential of an inland waterway cutting across New York state. More than fifty years before him, an Irish-born scientist named Cadwallader Colden – who, in 1724, was surveyor general to the colonial governor of New York – proclaimed the military and economic value of the Hudson and Mohawk valleys; but the British had done nothing to take advantage of it. By connecting the Hudson River with Lake Erie, this waterway at last would breach the extensive mountain barrier that had divided the country, and effectively open up trade between the East and the West.

Four years after Morris's pep talk on the Hudson, the war for independence was won. Americans began heading for the western territories to find a piece of land of their own, and the stories they sent back East started the tide of emigration flowing. They told of land that raised a hundred bushels of corn to an acre; of hogs that grew wonderfully fat just rooting on acorns and beechnuts the forests provided at no cost to the settler; of the poorest families who "here adorn their tables three times a day like a wedding feast."

Farmers weary of fighting the rocks on thin-soiled hill farms in New England, and others in cities crowded with people but few prospects, heard the call and headed west. But as of yet, there were no lines of covered wagons along this westward route, because most of the mountain crossings were trails just wide enough for a traveler on horseback, followed by a pack horse and perhaps two or three cattle.

The way west was difficult. The long chain of the Appalachian Mountains extending from Canada into Alabama formed a wall dividing the country in half. Eastern manufacturers had no way of shipping their goods to people living across the mountains except at tremendous cost. And faced with the same difficulties of transportation, the western farmers had no incentive to grow crops for the big eastern cities.

The great need was for a new and easy road through the mountains. But in all the hundreds of miles of mountain country between the gap cut by the St. Lawrence River, and Alabama, where the mountains dwindle away, there is only one real break - the valley where the Mohawk and the

Hudson rivers meet. This gap was an ancient Indian way, and then an early route of fur men, used and fought over by Dutch, French, English, and Americans. But, while this was a way through the mountains, it was by no means a smooth and easy route.

The Hudson River part of the route was all a traveler could ask for; nature had made it deep and wide and calm, with little current. The Mohawk was another story. It was dangerous in high water and impassable in low. Even when a boatman caught it right, there were parts of the river a boat could never get through: There were swirling rapids, foaming waterfalls, and passages choked with rocks.

Navigation on the Mohawk was completely barred near its mouth by Cohoes Falls, also called "The Great Falls." This prevented the traveler who took a Hudson River boat to the juncture of the two rivers from changing to another boat to continue up the Mohawk. He had to load his family and possessions aboard a wagon at Albany, and then rattle for seventeen miles over the rough trail to Schenectady, where the Mohawk became a little tamer. There he hired a square-ended, flat-bottomed bateau – a shallow-draft boat - and boatmen to pole them up the river.

About fifty-five miles west of Schenectady, another cataract, Little Falls, forced a mile-long portage. There, everyone got out while the bateau was hauled around the waterfalls - people of the village earned a good part of their living performing that service for boatmen. Then the backbreaking work of poling against the current began again. When the river became too narrow or shallow for the boat, another wagon was hired, and the westbound family rattled overland to Lake Ontario. There they took another lake boat as far as the Niagara River, where there was more land travel to get around the falls and rapids. Then at Buffalo, everybody piled aboard a Lake Erie boat and crossed into the west.

Even with these tremendous difficulties, this was one of the favored ways to go west, and the number of people moving along it steadily increased.

"A Canal to the Moon"

There were many half-formed plans for improving the waterway. The plan with the most potential to succeed was presented in 1784 by an engineering genius named Christopher Colles, who had already designed a water distribution system for New York City that utilized pipes made from hollowed logs. Speaking to a committee of the New York State legislature, Colles proposed a project to improve navigation on the Mohawk River. "By this," he asserted, "the internal trade will be increased . . . the country will be settled . . . the frontiers will be secured." He believed that it would be possible to travel strictly by boat from the Hudson River to Lake Ontario, and possibly Lake Erie.

The legislators were impressed by the plan, though not enough to finance it. Instead, they authorized him to conduct his own study, and promised a share of the profits from tolls should it prove fruitful. Six months later, the New York government paid Colles $125 (equal to about $2,250 today) to look into the cost and challenges of clearing obstacles to boat traffic along the Mohawk. But, failing to raise enough money privately to launch a viable company, Colles was forced to abandon the project – with nothing to show for his efforts.

In 1788, another visionary, Elkanah Watson arrived in New York on a sightseeing trip up the Mohawk River valley and made his own prediction. Born in Plymouth, Massachusetts, the thirty-year-old Watson had traveled all over Europe. During the Revolutionary War, he had carried dispatches from America to Benjamin Franklin (who became a close friend) in France, and later had explored England, Italy, and the Low Countries. He had also seen much of the eastern United States, from Massachusetts to Florida. But, in the wilderness north of Albany, he was overcome by "the majestic appearance of the adjacent mountains, the state of advanced agriculture . . . and the rich fragancy of the air, redolent with the perfume of the clover," which he wrote, "all combined to present a scene . . . [I was] not prepared to witness." During this trip, Watson later claimed, he first envisioned that "a canal communication will be opened, sooner or later, between the great lakes and the Hudson."

Watson was inspired by canals in Europe – particularly northwest England's Bridgewater Canal. Commissioned by the Duke of Bridgewater to transport coal from his mines in Worsley to Manchester, the canal was built between 1759 and 1761 at a cost of 168,000 pounds (equal to more than $33 billion today). Its most spectacular feature was an aqueduct, or water-carrying bridge, supported by three great arches that carried the canal across the River Irwell. The canal also ran underground for forty-six miles, as deep as four miles, through the mines so that coal could be loaded directly onto the boats. That convenience led to a more than

50-percent drop in coal prices in the canal's first year, which paid huge dividends to the Duke of Bridgewater. Observing its operation, a decade later, Watson summed up the ingenuity of the canal builders: "Not content with skimming along the surface, with traversing valleys and crossing rivers by their artificial navigation, they decided to plunge into the very bowels of a mountain, in pursuit of coal."

Convinced that Albany, New York, could be the hub of such activity, he moved there in 1789 and began to invest in land and businesses. Two years later, with some influential friends, Watson traveled up the Mohawk River on a six-week survey and reported his findings to the New York State legislature. Observing salt manufacturing near present-day Onondaga Lake, he wrote: "These works are in a rude, unfinished state – but are capable of making about eight thousand bushels of salt per annum; which is nearly the quantity required for the present consumption of the country. . . . Providence has happily placed this great source of comfort, and wealth, precisely in a position accessible by water in every direction. . . . When the mighty canals shall be formed and locks erected, it will add vastly to the facility of an extended diffusion, and the increase of intrinsic worth."

But in December 1791, he believed that travel from the Hudson to the Great Lakes would have to rely on the natural waterways because a manmade canal of that size was cost prohibitive. "The utmost stretch of our views," he later admitted about his thinking at this time, "was to follow the track of Nature's canal [rivers and lakes] and to remove natural or artificial obstructions; but we never entertained the most distant conception of a canal from Lake Erie to the Hudson. We should have considered it not much more extravagant to have suggested the possibility of a canal to the moon."

The possibilities began to expand the next year. Watson's influential friends included Philip Schuyler - the U.S. Senator from New York, and a canal enthusiast who also had paid close attention to the effects of the Bridgewater Canal on England. Schuyler was just the sort of man who could get a canal project started: A wealthy property owner; a hero of the Revolutionary War; and father-in-law of Alexander Hamilton, the first United States Secretary of the Treasury. And get it started, he did.

Watson made a copy of his report, stating the case for a waterway to the Great Lakes, which Schuyler passed among New York's legislators. Albany newspapers also published articles written by Watson, sometimes anonymously, on the virtues of canals. In the spring of 1792, as Schuyler had promised, a canal bill was brought before the New York State legislature, and passed. With the Mohawk Improvement Bill and subsequent acts, New York incorporated two private canal companies: the Northern Inland Lock Navigation Company (to build a waterway from the Hudson to Lake Champlain) and the Western Inland Lock Navigation Company (to improve navigation of the Mohawk River to Lake Ontario). Governor George Clinton, who had co-sponsored the bill, called for the companies to be given "every fostering aid and patronage;" and Senator Schuyler was made president of both.

The patronage of the state of New York, however, was not enough. The state paid each of the canal companies $12,500 (equal to more than $300,000 today). Each company was also authorized to sell 1,000 shares to the public, at $25 per share, to start with – for a total capital of $50,000 (more than $1.2 million today) between the two projects. The state gave Schuyler fifteen years to complete the work. But shareholders were not easy to come by - after three days in which not a single share was sold, Elkanah Watson was despondent. "I considered the cause hopeless," he said, until he was able to convince a friend to buy twenty shares. "From that moment," he said, "subscriptions went on briskly." Many of the shareholders were wealthy businessmen from New York; some were farmers who owned property along the proposed waterways and thus stood to benefit from the projects. Within two years, the Western Company would sell 743 of its 1,000 shares, and the Northern Company 676 – but nearly 500 of those would be forfeited because of missed payments by the shareholders. Even as state aid and demands on shareholders increased, there was never enough money.

In the spring of 1793, the Northern Company began to dig a canal from Stillwater to Waterford in upstate New York, but the work was stopped because of a lack of funds. Soon after, the company went bankrupt.

Around the same time, the Western Company started work to improve the Mohawk River to Lake Ontario. In the next several years, a canal was cut through the rocks around Little Falls, a mile more was dug to bypass another bad spot, and a channel and locks were completed, connecting the Mohawk with Wood Creek.

Locks, a fixed chamber with gates at both ends in which water levels can be varied to raise and lower boats, were first used in medieval China during the tenth century. But the design adopted by Europe and then the United States – and still in use today – was created by Renaissance man Leonardo da Vinci, who in the late fifteenth and early sixteenth centuries was obsessed with the movement of water. In 1485, his design was used to build the eighteen locks of the Bereguardo Canal in Italy, which raised and lowered boats eighty feet over twelve miles from Milan to Pavia. Da Vinci had the idea for the gates, when closed, to form a "V" pointing upstream so that the pressure of the water current keeps them tightly sealed. Sluices, or slots, in the gates then let water in or out of the locks to raise or lower the boat. When the boat reaches the level of the stream it is entering, the gates open and the boat proceeds.

On the Mohawk, five locks were built, over a distance of about a mile - each one raising or lowering boats by nine feet. That work made it possible to go by boat from the Mohawk, through the chain of lakes in central and western New York, to within a few miles of the Pennsylvania line. It also cut travel time at this juncture from a day to about an hour. But the locks were poorly constructed – first from wood that rotted and later from brick and stone that lacked a double mortar – and leaked.

At first, the company dug and blasted with a great deal of enthusiasm. About 300 men were employed as laborers. But soon both money and enthusiasm were gone. A canal around the massive Cohoes Falls was too much even to attempt, it was decided, and goods still had to be transshipped from the Mohawk to the Hudson. In the end, the rough and rocky Mohawk River was not much changed.

The work was crude and only partly finished, but it gave a

hint of what a real waterway along this route would mean. Before that time, shallow boats capable of carrying a ton and a half of cargo were the largest that could be used on the Mohawk, simply because heavier boats could not be dragged around Little Falls. But with the locks, flatboats called Durham boats - as long as sixty feet and carrying sixteen tons of cargo - could easily be floated past the waterfalls. A bateau could carry only one emigrant family and its possessions, but several families along with their wagons, plows, kettles, and Bibles could ride on a Durham boat. As a result, boatmen were able to lower their fares, and the freight rates dropped correspondingly. This further increased westward travel through the Mohawk Valley and sparked interest in an even cheaper and easier route inland.

The Western Inland Lock Navigation Company, however, was not going to be the one to build that better way. The company had used every cent it had collected in tolls just to keep its shaky locks and channels in working condition. Stockholders were called on again and again to pay extra assessments. But in eighteen years, the company had not been able to return a single penny to the investors who had put their money into it expecting a good profit. Finally, in 1810, the company went to the state of New York for help, but was refused.

"If We Must Have War, or a Canal . . ."

A prominent politician named Jonas Platt – then a New York state senator and leader of the state's Federalist Party - had decided that it was time the state itself got things moving. He wanted to build a canal right across the state. With his friend Thomas Eddy, treasurer of the failed Western Inland Lock Navigation Company, Platt looked into two possible canal routes – one to Lake Ontario and one to Lake Erie.

In 1809, New York sent two legislators to Washington to talk with President Thomas Jefferson about financial help from the federal government for the canal. They knew that Jefferson had proposed spending federal funds on building roads and canals, and they hoped to convince him of the importance of the Erie project. But Jefferson had a pet canal project of his own. He was thinking of the Potomac Company, which had been formed in 1785 with George Washington as its president.

The Potomac Company had planned to build a canal from the capital of Washington across the Appalachians to the Ohio River. George Washington had understood the importance of connecting the East and West; he feared constantly that, separated by natural barriers, the western settlers might break from the United States to form their own nation. But the Potomac Company had run out of money after it had done no more than build a canal to bypass the worst of the Potomac rapids, which foamed over rock ledges near Washington.

President Jefferson still held out hope that the early canal project might be finished. He also believed that the proposed New York canal was impractical - too long and far too difficult to construct in 1809. "It is a splendid project and may be executed a century hence," the president remarked to the two New Yorkers, ". . . but it is little short of madness to think of it at this day!"

Badly as the canal wanted federal funds, it needed a local champion even more. The men who needed political support to get action on the canal turned finally to a man named De Witt Clinton. Forty-three-year-old Clinton was mayor of New York City, and the Democratic leader of the state. He had served in the state legislature and then in the United States Senate before becoming one of the most active mayors New York City would ever have. When there was a fire, he arrived at the scene behind his own galloping team almost as soon as the first fire wagon, and he showed up to help the police when there was any disturbance. He was also a member of many philosophical organizations and an ardent naturalist.

The only trouble was that De Witt Clinton had never been much interested in the canal, nor had he really given much thought to it. But his chief political opponent, Jonas Platt, who had been lobbying for the canal, knew that the project had little chance without Clinton's support. Fortunately, Platt realized that the waterway was more important than political maneuvering, and he suggested that Clinton take the lead in backing it. Clinton saw that such a move might be politically advantageous, and threw his support behind the project. "From that period," wrote Platt, "Mr. Clinton devoted the best powers of his vigorous and capacious mind to this subject; and he appeared to grasp and realize it, as an object of the highest public utility, and worthy of his noblest ambition." No one worked harder for the canal than he did. In fact, the Erie Canal might never have been dug if it had not been for the ceaseless efforts of De Witt Clinton.

By 1810, an Erie Canal was out of the dream stage, and a committee was appointed to study the problems of digging the canal. Clinton, of course, was made one of the seven commissioners. Gouverneur Morris - getting a little gray by now, but still vigorous and full of ideas – was appointed president of the group, but the title was mainly ceremonial; everyone looked to Clinton for leadership. The bipartisan Erie Canal Commission was equally divided between Federalists and Democrats. Its other members included Thomas Eddy, geographer and surveyor Simeon DeWitt, and Stephen Van Rensselaer (heir to one of New York's largest estates, and the tenth richest American of all time).

The commissioners traveled into the wilds of western New York to look over the path of the proposed canal. Except for Rensselaer and Morris, who took a carriage the whole way, they went by boat as far as they could up the Mohawk. The trip – more than 700 miles from Albany to Lake Erie and back – took the commissioners fifty-three days. De Witt Clinton chronicled it in detail in his journal, 170 pages in all, including precise records of the mileage between points as well as colorful notes on the geography, people, and wildlife they encountered.

Departing Schenectady in a shallow bateau, Clinton wrote: "These boats are not sufficiently safe for lake navigation, although they frequently venture. . . . After sailing a couple of miles, a bend of the river brought the wind in our faces. Our men took to their poles, and pushed us up against a rapid current with great dexterity, and great muscular exertion."

The natural obstacles became more pronounced at the Little Falls, where Clinton observed, "the river becomes narrow and deep, and you pass through immense rocks, principally of granite, interspersed with limestone. . . . In all directions, you behold great rocks, exhibiting rotundities, points, and cavities, as if worn by the violence of the waves or pushed from their former positions." There, they saw the deteriorating state of the locks built more than a decade before by the Western Inland Lock Navigation Company. Clinton criticized that effort as "worse than useless," blaming the inexperience of its superintendent Philip Schuyler, and boasting that a better job could be done for less than half of what it had cost the Western Company.

From this survey, Clinton and the others became convinced that the canal must be completely artificial, to avoid the natural hazards of streams and rivers. The Western Company's failure to tame the Mohawk River – the most practical east-west route – was evidence enough.

Back in Albany in late August 1810, the commissioners began the intimidating job of sorting through their notes and coming to a consensus on a canal plan. In the six months it took them to prepare their report, they could have made the trip from Albany to Lake Erie three times. The biggest holdup was over the route the canal would take. Commissioner Peter Buell Porter - a businessman with a monopoly on trade in Black Rock (now Buffalo), in northwest New York – had a lot to gain by diverting the canal through that area and Lake Ontario. Throughout the entire process, Porter unabashedly pursued his own self-interests. But eventually, it was agreed by all that the canal had to run straight to Lake Erie. At Lake Ontario, the canal would have to compete with the St. Lawrence River - drawing western traders east through Montreal, Canada, all the way to the Atlantic

Ocean, and bypassing New York. The Lake Erie route would make the Hudson River and New York the main trade artery. The route to Lake Erie was longer, but it also avoided the barrier of Niagara Falls.

Finally in March 1811, the committee submitted its report to the New York legislature, recommending that the waterway run beside the Mohawk River only as far as Utica and from there continue on to Lake Erie in its own path. The committee first suggested an inclined plane - a canal without locks which would slope gently downhill all the way from Lake Erie to Utica. This slope, according to the plan, would provide just enough slant to keep the water running and the channel full, but not enough to make it difficult to tow a boat against the current.

The inclined plane was Gouverneur Morris's idea, but simple as it appeared, the plan proved too impractical to build. It would have required great embankments to carry it over the low places; and at one spot, it would have needed a tremendous aqueduct - 150 feet high - to carry the waterway across a particularly low area. Arguments had been made in committee meetings, but Morris remained adamant, and De Witt Clinton urged everyone to sign off on the inclined plane plan, though he did not believe in it himself. Clinton believed it was most important to present a unified message to the legislature, to keep the canal project from stalling, and that common sense would eventually prevail. He was right.

New York legislators were so impressed by the report that on April 8, 1811, they passed the first of many laws related to the building of the canal. Hudson River steamboat developer Robert Fulton and his engineering partner, Robert R. Livingston, were added to the Erie Canal Commission. The state also allocated $15,000 to get the canal project started. One important stipulation made by the commission was that the canal should be publicly funded; by avoiding private interests, the state could maintain control. Given the authority to take whatever steps necessary, the commission members set out to secure the money.

There was still hope that the federal government would help foot the bill. Clinton and Morris went to Washington to try to convince Jefferson's successor, James Madison, that the nation – not just New York – stood to benefit greatly from the canal. De Witt Clinton had an advantage: His uncle George Clinton was Madison's vice president. But once again, the canal project failed to gain any federal support. Renewed hostilities with Britain would turn a $6.3 million federal surplus in 1811 into a $10.5 million deficit by the next year, as the United States girded for war. Clinton and Morris had an ingenious solution for the cash-poor government: If it would just grant the commission federal lands out west, in the Indian Territory, they could sell those lands to raise money for the canal. Still, the answer was no. This was just the first of many setbacks for the Erie Canal.

Much of the public reaction to the canal plan also was cold. Many believed the scope was just too large to pull off; others were proud that their young nation could even attempt a project of such imposing size. The overall incredulity made it difficult for the commission to secure land grants from property owners along the proposed canal route.

Early in 1812, it was estimated that the construction of an inclined plane would cost between $5 million and $6 million (the equivalent of between $87 million and $105 million today). Hopeful attempts to obtain loans in England and France were made, but they failed, and Morris's scheme was dropped. Then Clinton and the other commissioners sat down and started to work on plans for a canal with locks – which would be considerably cheaper to build than an inclined plane. In June, the Erie Canal Commission took a big step in buying the rights, interests, and estate of the Western Inland Lock Navigation Company.

But the canal troubles of 1812 were not over yet. War broke out with Great Britain on June 18, 1812 - dimming hopes for pushing the immediate construction of the canal.

Not only did it divert crucial resources, the War of 1812 coincided with a presidential election, which divided the attention and interests of the country, as well as the canal commission. De Witt Clinton ran for President of the United States on an anti-war platform that appealed to both Federalists and a small group of Democrats. He lost in a close race to incumbent James Madison. The election also caused a rift between Clinton and New York Governor Daniel Tompkins, who had been a friend, but had chosen to back Madison for president. The support of the New York State Legislature waned, too. After voting in 1812 to allow the Erie Canal Commission to create a fund for financing the project, the legislature repealed the act in 1814.

The war, however, did emphasize the need for a good waterway: The rotting old locks built by the Western Inland

Lock Navigation Company could barely handle the heavy war traffic. When the war ended on February 18, 1815, in a military stalemate and with no changes to United States boundaries, attention was redirected to the canal project.

Unfortunately, the war also gave canal opponents time to gather their forces. New York City politicians stubbornly opposed the upstate project, though common sense should have told them that the commerce brought by the canal could only increase the greatness of their city. Then there were people in the Lake Ontario counties who wanted the canal to end at Oswego on Lake Ontario, instead of going on to Lake Erie and opening east-west traffic. And there were the farmers near the Pennsylvania border who saw no reason to pay taxes to help build a waterway so far away from them. But Clinton, always the master politician, promised to run branch canals into other parts of the state and soon had most of the farmers on his side.

Still, many grumbled there was no chance that a canal 363 miles long could be dug successfully through all that wilderness. Look, they said, at the Western Inland Lock Navigation Company, which had tried to carry out a much less ambitious program but had been able to complete only a small part of it before it went broke. Another sad example was the Middlesex Canal, which ran twenty-seven miles from Boston to the Merrimack River. The longest canal in the country, the Middlesex was a marvel to shippers bringing New Hampshire granite and lumber to Boston markets. But it was a nightmare to its owners, who had to dig into their pockets again and again to pay off its debts. If a twenty-seven-mile canal near busy Boston went broke, asked the critics of the Erie, what chance was there for a ditch that would run hundreds of miles through the wilds of upper New York State?

In spite of the opposition, pressure for the canal was building. New England farmers, dreaming about taking up a piece of easily plowed land in the Indiana or Illinois territories, were fascinated by the prospect of gliding along a smooth waterway rather than wearing out horses and axles on a miserable, potholed road over the mountains. Eastern merchants were ready to sell axes, buttons, plowpoints, cloth, fox traps, and a thousand other things to western settlers as soon as economical transportation was available.

On December 3, 1815, canal commissioners called a public meeting at the City Hotel in New York City to try to win over their most vocal detractors. Jonas Platt, now a New York State Supreme Court justice, helped to organize the meeting, and invitations were sent out to about 100 prominent city leaders. The turnout was better than expected, as a crowd overflowed the meeting hall. De Witt Clinton was the principal speaker, reading from a document he had written called the "New York Memorial."

In this statement, to be presented to the state legislature, Clinton included details of cost estimates, toll projections, and ideas about the design of the canal. Playing to his audience, he talked up New York's superiority over its competitors as an artery to the west. He spoke at length about the variety of crops and merchandise that would be transported. The canal, he said, would "convey more riches on its waters than any other canal in the world," and New York City would be transformed into "the great depot and warehouse of the western world."

More than just a boon to New York, the canal was vital to strengthening the United States, Clinton said. Raising the value of "national domains" along the canal route would facilitate the repayment of national debt, and free up resources "to be expended in great public improvements; in encouraging the arts and sciences; in patronizing the operations of industry; in fostering the inventions of genius; and in diffusing the blessing of knowledge. . . ." But the canal's greatest contribution, he argued, would be to defend the young nation from its "most imminent danger": "A line of separation, may be eventually drawn between the Atlantic and the western states, unless they are cemented by a common, an ever acting, and a powerful interest."

The canal champion insisted that fast action was needed. "Delays are the refuge of weak minds," he said, "and to procrastinate on this occasion is to show a culpable inattention to the bounties of nature; a total insensibility to the blessings of Providence, and an inexcusable neglect of the interests of society. . . . The overflowing blessings from this great fountain of public good and national abundance, will be as extensive as our country and as durable as time. . . . It remains for a free state to create a new era in history, and to erect a work more stupendous, more magnificent, and more beneficial than has hitherto been achieved by the human race."

The speech was extremely persuasive; soon, copies of it were being distributed across the state. As one newspaper writer reported, "it produced an electrical effect throughout the whole country."

Throughout 1816, in almost every town and village along

the route of the proposed canal, mass meetings were held to demand that the lawmakers in Albany do whatever was necessary to get the work started. Many citizens of New York City and other parts of the state – more than 100,000 people in all - signed petitions asking for the same canal their own representatives were opposing. "Our tables have groaned with the petitions of these people," said Martin Van Buren, then a U.S. Senator from New York and later President of the United States. At first against the canal, Van Buren changed his stance and threw his support behind a bill to sell state bonds to raise money for the project.

Capitalizing on that momentum, the Erie Canal Commission, formed two years before, submitted its final report to the New York State Legislature on March 8, 1816: "From the number and respectability of the applications now before the legislature in favor of an immediate commencement and vigorous prosecution of this great national work, it is evident that the immense advantages which would result from its completion are duly appreciated by our fellow-citizens, and it only remains for the legislature to sanction by their approval an undertaking which combines in one object the honor, interest, and political eminence of the state." The report recommended a search to find and employ the best American engineers so that the work on the canal could begin in earnest.

After many debates and amendments, a bill was passed April 17 that created a new canal commission, with De Witt Clinton again as president. Appropriating $20,000 for new studies, the commission's mission was "to consider, devise, and adopt such measures as may or shall be required to facilitate and effect the communication, by means of canals and locks, between the navigable waters of Hudson's rivers and Lake Erie, and the said navigable waters and Lake Champlain." But it was another year before the legislature voted to authorize the construction of the canal.

In the meantime, others were lining up to tout the benefits of a canal. Despite being labeled by Clinton as a critic of the canal project, New York Governor Tompkins spoke out in favor of it. Addressing a session of the state legislature, Tompkins said: "It will rest with Legislature whether the prospect of connecting the waters of the Hudson with those of the western lakes and Champlain is not sufficiently important to demand the appropriation of some part of the revenues of the state to its accomplishments, without imposing too great a burden upon our constituents." Clinton charged that this was a change of heart, motivated purely by politics, since it was now becoming popular to support the canal.

Tompkins was preparing to take a run at becoming President of the United States, and he had the support of many New Yorkers. But the Democratic Party instead chose James Monroe as its nominee, and Tompkins as his running mate. In the 1816 election, the Monroe-Tompkins ticket won by a wide margin over Federalist candidate Rufus King, the United States senator from New York.

With Tompkins elected Vice President, New York called a special election to choose a new governor in the spring of 1817. De Witt Clinton was the only candidate. But Clinton's political enemies – members of the influential, and largely Irish-Catholic, society known as Tammany Hall – printed ballots in New York City that listed an opponent: Peter Buell Porter. As a member of the canal commission with Clinton, Porter had been thwarted in his attempt to run the canal through his lands in Black Hills and then Lake Ontario. He hated Clinton, but he represented no real political threat. The ballot initiative amounted to no more than a protest, with Porter as a sort of write-in candidate; it was Tammany Hall's way of going on record with their gripes against Clinton. But in the end, Clinton was elected governor, with 43,310 votes to Porter's 1,479 votes – the most lopsided victory in New York history. In voting for Clinton and his political allies, who had made the canal a major issue in their campaign, the people were really voting for the canal itself.

Later that year, when the all-important bill for funds to build the canal came up in the state legislature, its enemies still fought hard. Not until the final hour of the session did the bill come to a vote and pass. One of the most moving appeals was made, just prior to the vote, by Elisha Williams, a Federalist and the representative for the District of Columbia, who said: "If the canal is to be a shower of gold, it will fall upon New York; if a river of gold, it will flow into her lap."

But even then, the battle was not quite over. Under the rules of the New York Legislature, the bill had to be approved by a special group called the Council of Revision. Two of the five members were firmly opposed to the idea of a canal.

Lieutenant Governor John Tayler, acting as the council's president, "panted with honest zeal to strangle the infant Hercules at its birth, by his casting vote in the negative," according to Judge Jonas Platt, the council member leading the push for the canal. Smith Thompson, chief justice of the New York State Supreme Court, wanted the canal to be privately funded and controlled – a point that was roundly dismissed – and so voted no. Another justice on the state Supreme Court, Joseph C. Yates "was a decided friend of the canal, and voted for the bill," recounted Platt. The deciding vote seemed to belong to James Kent, chancellor of New York (the highest judicial officer in the state). Kent thought the canal might be a fine thing someday - but not for a good many years in the future.

The great waterway seemed doomed when Vice President Tompkins walked into the meeting room of the divided council.

De Witt Clinton had been right about Tompkins, who, now that he was no longer running for office, was looking to undermine the canal project. The vice president considered the canal a waste of money. In an attempt to sway the vote, he warned council members that there would be another war with England within two years, and that the state ought to be spending its money on weapons and fortifications, rather than for anything as foolish as the canal.

As it turned out, that was the worst thing he could have said. Chancellor Kent, who was going to vote against the canal bill, resented Tompkins's attempts to frighten the committee with talk of war. Rising from his seat, Kent announced, "If we must have war, or have a canal, I am in favor of the canal."

And so, by the margin of one vote, the Erie Canal was approved. It was one of the most important votes in American history. The crowd of people waiting outside in a hard April rain to hear the decision knew how important it was, and cheered again and again when the final vote was announced. Jonas Platt wrote about the victory: "If that bill had been rejected by the council, it could not have been carried by two-thirds of the Senate and Assembly. . . . At no future period could the work have been accomplished at so small an expense of land, of water, and hydraulic privileges. Rival routes, and local interests, were daily increasing and combining against the project; and in my estimation it was one of the chief grounds of merit in the advocates of the Erie Canal that they seized on the very moment most proper and auspicious for that immortal work."

Now the job was up to the men with axes and picks and shovels.

2

DIGGING THE DITCH

On July 4, 1817, at the head of the Mohawk River, in the wilderness village of Rome, the Erie Canal at last got under way with a ceremony to mark the turning of the first shovelfuls of earth.

Just after sunrise on a day chosen to symbolize national unity, Samuel Young began the proceedings with a short speech, in which he prophesied: "By this great highway, unborn millions will easily transport their surplus productions to the shores of the Atlantic, procure their supplies, and hold a useful and profitable intercourse with all the maritime nations of the world." Young, previously Speaker of the New York State Assembly, had been named to the Erie Canal Commission the year before.

Other dignitaries said their few words; then, a cannon boomed to signal a plow tied to a team of oxen that had been waiting off to the side. Driving the plow was John Richardson, who eight days earlier had been the first contractor signed to the canal project. Richardson was a veteran of two American wars, a cabinet maker, and the first judge of the Court of Common Pleas of Cayuga County, New York. As the plow dug into ground, marked by a line of stakes, that was destined to become part of the great waterway to the west, the dignitaries each in turn took a bright new spade and scooped up a bit of dirt. The crowd of onlookers cheered, cannons boomed, the crowd cheered again, and construction on the great western canal was officially begun. Now the real work could start.

Rome, at first glance, might seem an odd place to start digging a canal. It was out on the edge of nowhere, with only three or four tiny settlements and a tremendous amount of wilderness between it and Lake Erie to the west. And there was a considerable amount of wilderness to the east as well. Materials and tools would have to be hauled into Rome over difficult trails and waterways, or fashioned on the spot. But it was the town nearest the upper limit of navigation on the Mohawk River. It was also right at the middle section of the canal – strategically important because it linked eastern and western New York State. Once completed, it would provide a shorter, smoother route than the one from Lake Ontario, through Canada, on the St. Lawrence River.

Here, the digging also would be the easiest. There was little rock to cut through at Rome, and it was level country where no locks would be needed for at least sixty miles.

De Witt Clinton, who just three days before the ceremony at Rome had taken the oath of office as New York's governor, believed it was important to make good progress at the beginning, to have something to show the people as soon as possible. Had work begun from the Hudson River end, there would have been rocks to blast through and locks to build from the start. In spite of all the blueprints and brave talk, no one knew enough about canal building yet to begin on such a difficult segment.

The canal commissioners had decided that the canal would be built in three sections: 165 miles from Lake Erie to the Seneca River; seventy-two miles from the Seneca to Rome; and the steep, 126-mile downward slope from Rome to Albany, on the Hudson River. Because it would be the simplest to engineer, the middle section was also certain to be the cheapest – at about $1.5 million, according to projections. The commissioners' report to the legislature estimated the total cost of the canal project at $4.9 million – which worked out to about $13,400 per mile. By comparison, George Washington's abandoned effort to build canals around the rapids of the Potomac River had run around $300,000, while the Western Inland Lock Navigation Company had spent about $400,000 to build poor locks over little more than a mile of the Mohawk River.

From end to end, Hudson River to Lake Erie, the canal would be 363 miles long. The channel was to be forty feet wide at the surface, and would slope inward to twenty-eight feet at the bottom; the water in the channel would be four feet deep. Besides these basic requirements, the engineers would have to consider that Lake Erie is 568 feet higher than the Hudson River. There were also places where the canal would step down to cross a broad valley and then rise up again on the other side. So, counting steps up and down, the total vertical distance a boat would travel on the canal would be 688 feet. Eighty-three locks, each ninety feet long and fifteen feet wide, would have to be built to overcome these differences in height.

There were other problems: American canal boats had neither sails nor oars, and needed to be towed. So, along the length of the canal, there would be a towpath ten feet wide for the horses and mules which were needed to draw the canal boats. Few sections of the Erie Canal could run through any existing stream, and uncontrollable natural waterways had to be avoided completely. Where the channel ran next to the Mohawk River, it would be carefully protected from it by walls and dikes. These and a thousand other things had to be planned carefully before construction could begin.

As though these engineering feats were not enough, the legislature of New York also approved the digging of a canal from Lake Champlain to the Hudson River. It would join the Erie Canal near the Hudson end of their courses, where the combined traffic would move down to Albany and on to the Hudson River. The Champlain Canal was projected to cost $900,000. Cautious men shook their heads at the mounting costs, while the project's most vehement opponents grinned slyly and then sat back to wait for the whole mad canal scheme to collapse and bury Clinton's political hopes once and for all.

But up around Rome, activity on the Erie Canal was well under way. Surveyors first had staked out a sixty-foot-wide path to be cleared of trees; within this were set two rows of stakes, forty feet apart, to mark the actual channel. Next came the axemen to clear the sixty-foot swath. This was truly a job for the legendary woodsman, Paul Bunyan. The men had to clear mile after mile of woods, and fell trees, many of which were seven or eight feet in diameter.

Once the trees and brush were down and burned, the crews with shovels had their turn. These men had to dig through a tangled mass of roots which nature had been weaving into a nearly impregnable barrier for centuries. It not only took courage to face such difficulties, but a touch of madness as well, for no one then had had any real experience in building such a canal.

Not just experience was lacking; there was no precedent in all history for a canal of the Erie's length. Canal building was a young and undeveloped art. True, it had been practiced by the Egyptians, who had constructed canals of up to 125 miles in length before the birth of Christ. But the Egyptian canals generally ran over level terrain, involved a ruthless expenditure of human life, and were often little more than impermanent ditches. What knowledge the Egyptians, and later the Romans and Chinese, acquired in the building of canals was buried, as were most of the canals themselves, in the Middle Ages. Only in the seventeenth century, with the development of the locks in Italy, was the art revived, and then the first true ancestors of the Erie Canal were born.

The largest European canal to grow out of the revival was the Languedoc Canal that cut across southern France, connecting the Atlantic with the Mediterranean. Still in operation – renamed Canal du Midi ("Canal of the Two Seas") in 1789 – the 144-mile waterway has 119 locks, and is a complex of aqueducts and tunnels as well as channels. Opened in 1681, it was still considered a marvel of modern engineering when the Erie's planners were brashly contemplating a canal two and a half times as long.

Planners of the Erie Canal also were inspired by a rash of canals built in England in the second half of the eighteenth century. William Weston, an English engineer who had gained his experience in this building spree, had been hired by the Western Lock Navigation Company to aid their abortive efforts to build a canal linking the Hudson and Lake Ontario. The Erie commissioners tried to get Weston for their ambitious undertaking, offering him the handsome salary of $7,000 a year (equal to about $118,000 today). But in 1817, Weston was fifty-four years old, and in poor health. He turned down the job offer, but wished the commissioners well and predicted that their "noble and stupendous plan . . . [would] have to fear no rivalry."

The commissioners instead selected two New York lawyers, Benjamin Wright and James Geddes, to be the chief engineers on the canal. It was a gamble, because their only previous experience had been some surveying work tied to legal cases involving property boundaries. But there was no list of canal engineers to choose from. Though Wright and Geddes were not engineers by profession, the commissioners felt that the two men were competent and intelligent enough to solve the problems of canal construction on the job. In the end, the commissioners turned out to be right.

Wright and Geddes were meticulous in their designs, and not having worked together before, cooperated well. Born in Connecticut, Wright had arrived in Rome, New York, in 1789 at age nineteen; he had served on the New York State Legislature and as a county judge. Geddes, the son of a Scottish farmer, was from Pennsylvania, where he had worked briefly as a schoolmaster. He first arrived in New York in 1793, to work for a salt manufacturer outside of Syracuse on Onondaga Lake, where in 1807 he founded the village of Geddes, named after him.

The engineers' first test on the Erie Canal project was to survey the summit near Rome, where the Mohawk River rises to begin its eastward journey toward Albany. The stakes were high - according to one commissioner, a bad measurement of the elevation here would cause "irrevocable damnation." But any worries proved unwarranted. In their report, the commissioners praised Wright and Geddes for their "versatile ingenuity [and] degree of care, skill, and precision in the delicate art of leveling," which they said "had perhaps never been exceeded." They were so precise that, taking separate readings of one long stretch, starting on opposite ends, the difference was within two inches.

Responsibility for the canal was divided by section. Wright was assigned to the middle section, which was the first to get under way. Geddes would lead the western section from the Seneca to Lake Erie. A third engineer, Charles Broadhead, was hired to survey the eastern section from Rome to the Hudson. But after completing his report, Broadhead left the project, and Wright took over that section, too.

Each engineer had his own team of assistants, whose talents would contribute greatly to the project. On Wright's team, twenty-seven-year-old Canvass White was an amateur engineer, but his real skill lay in research. Convinced that further study of England's waterways could yield answers to the questions plaguing the Erie engineers, he traveled overseas – at his own expense - in 1817, and did not return until the following year. While there, he walked alongside 2,000 miles of English canals, paying attention to every detail. He brought back precise drawings of the canals, locks, aqueducts, dams, bridges and culverts – along with some of the latest surveying equipment being used in England. But a newfound knowledge of cement making turned out to be his greatest contribution.

White engaged in debates with Benjamin Wright and the other engineers on the best materials to use in constructing the locks and other submerged structures on the canal. Wood and brick, which on the Mohawk River had deteriorated within a few years, were ruled out. The English were using stone and a hydraulic cement mix made from trass, a volcanic rock which is rare in America and would have been too costly to import. So White set out to find a native material suitable for making cement. He found it not far from the Erie Canal route.

At quarries in Chittenango, in Madison County, White discovered a trass-like substance called meager limestone. After some experimenting, he developed a process to turn it into hydraulic cement by heating the limestone, pulverizing it into powder, and then adding it to sand and water. When cooled by the water, the cement solidified; over time, with continued exposure to water, it became even harder. He obtained a patent for his waterproof cement, which was both cheaper to make and better quality than what England had. Some 500,000 bushels of the cement would be used in the construction of the Erie Canal – for which White was paid nothing but compliments. Because the discovery was made during the course of White's work on the canal, the commissioners claimed ownership of it. Years later, White sued the State of New York for patent violations and settled for $10,000 ($250,000 today).

Other assistant engineers on the Erie project included Nathan S. Roberts, a genius of mathematics who, despite his own limited formal education, had become a schoolteacher in New Jersey by age sixteen. An itinerant teacher, moving from one community to the next, he used his wages to purchase 100 acres of land in Vermont and to do what he had always wanted to do: speculate in land sales. Benjamin Wright put Roberts in charge of thirteen men, surveying the canal route between Rome and Seneca Lake, which was accomplished in a little under a year, despite the terrible obstacles presented by what later became known as the Montezuma Swamp.

Roberts also took on an apprentice – twenty-two-year-old John B. Jervis, who was hired as an axeman on a construction team for the canal. Jervis learned fast, and eventually was put in charge of a fifty-mile section of the canal; later, he would go on to design and supervise the construction of early American railroads, which ironically would be the canal's undoing.

David Stanhope Bates was another assistant who would eventually distinguish himself as a pioneer of American civil engineering. Born on a farm near the St. Lawrence River - outside the village of Morristown, New York - Bates had been pushed by his father to pursue a career in ministry. But he was more interested in mathematics, which he studied while working as a clerk in his brother's store. He had some experience as a surveyor, having helped sell a large tract of land in Oneida County, New York, for a wealthy Scottish landowner in 1810. He had also been superintendent of the extensive Iron Works in the town of Rotterdam and, after studying law, a judge for the Oneida County Common Pleas Court. When he applied for a job on the canal, Benjamin Wright assigned Bates to the middle section.

The Erie Canal was the first American school of engineering - producing engineers who in their lifetimes covered the nation with their works of internal improvements. Charles Glidden Haines, personal secretary to Governor De Witt Clinton and a frequent contributor to New York newspapers on topics including the canal, would write in 1821: "For accuracy, dispatch, and science, we can now present a corps of engineers equal to any in the world."

But more than vision was needed to build a 363-mile canal. It required brawn, and lots of it.

"Through the Mire"

Finding workers for the canal was no problem. Men came from miles around, eager to make some of the big money being paid for diggers on the Big Ditch. First, the commissioners hired small-scale contractors, who agreed to dig a certain length of channel for a certain price. The canal commissioners wanted, as much as possible, contractors who were tied to the land – people who owned property along the canal route and would take pride in a job well done. In effect, each contractor was responsible for building his own small canal - often bounded by brooks and ravines, and thus separate from the canals of his neighbors on both sides.

It was then up to the contractor to hire the men to do the work. He was also expected to put up a shack big enough to sleep twenty-four to forty men; to supply them with horses, scrapers, shovels, and other equipment; to feed them and give them their daily ration of whiskey; and to pay them. Wages were as high as eighty cents a day. (By comparison, a New York state legislator was paid $3 a day.) Contracts stipulated that the contractor himself would not be paid until his section of the canal was complete, and had passed inspection by one of the engineers. But there were informal advances to cover expenses and the cost of materials and labor.

Many of the workers were local farmers, looking to improve their slack season by excavating a section of the ditch; some were Native Americans and freed slaves. Within six months of the groundbreaking at Rome, some fifty contractors had

1,000 men working on fifty-eight miles of the canal; and one fifteen-mile section was completed and had passed inspection. The results, Governor De Witt Clinton said, exceeded his "most sanguine expectations." By the summer of 1818, contracts were signed for the entire length of the canal, except for a few spots where aqueducts were necessary.

But with everyone shouting for more speed, the local workers were not enough. The farmers still had to tend to their own fields. Recruiters were sent down to New York City, to meet the immigrant boats arriving from Ireland. "Would they care for a fine job upstate?" the recruiters asked the husky young Irishmen. "We're digging a canal up there," they explained. "Working conditions are very good, with roast beef guaranteed twice a day, regular whiskey rations, and wages eighty cents." This was nearly twice as much as most unskilled laborers were earning in America at that time, and three times as much as unskilled immigrant laborers could have earned in Europe. By 1825, wages would rise to $1 a day. The Irish were ready to take almost any work; at these wages, it would have been impossible to keep them away.

The first of the Irish laborers arrived in 1818, and during the digging of the canal, they made up about a quarter of the work force. Soon they were joined by other European immigrants.

Everyone worked long, hard hours around the construction sites. In the Erie work camps, the wake-up horn was blown by the cook's helper half an hour before sunrise; he followed the blast with the call, "All out! Mush in the kettle!" There was more than mush; breakfast often included fried eggs, steak, sausage or pork chops, ham, potatoes, corn bread, rolls, batter cakes with molasses, buckwheat cakes with syrup, fried mush or mush-and-milk, and tea, coffee, or buttermilk. It took a lot of fuel to stoke up men for canal digging; they ate in a hurry and were at work by sun up.

The kitchen crew packed hearty lunches that the men carried along and ate at noon during a half-hour break. At night, they came in a little before sundown ready for a big supper. Game of every kind, from venison and bear to squirrel and partridge, was plentiful along the canal route, but the workers quickly grew tired of this woodland fare and demanded beef, pork, and mutton. Most contractors had to promise the men they hired that game would never be served to them more than a certain number of days in the week.

During the long days of summer, a work day might last as long as fourteen hours. After that, even a hard, board bunk probably felt good although the sleeping shacks provided scant comfort. There was no glass or screening on the windows, which meant every mosquito within miles could come and fill up on a canal-digger's blood. The two-tiered bunks had no mattresses; if a worker wanted bedding, he brought his own. The men had a saying: "Hickory lasts longer, but pine sleeps softer."

As the newness of the life wore off and the men got into the rhythm of their work, they sang a song of their own about the canal they were digging:

> We are cutting a Ditch through the gravel,
> Through the gravel across the state, by heck!
> We are cutting the Ditch through the gravel,
> So the people and the freight can travel,
> Can travel across the state, by heck!

And as they sang, the work began to go faster and more smoothly than it had at the beginning. Engineers and men alike had learned about canal building from scratch, but they learned fast. With the untrained improvisation that would become known as "Yankee ingenuity," they discovered how to lick problems that at first had made them shudder. Their only sources of power were the muscles of men, horses, and oxen, so they devised ways to increase their efficiency without adding to their work load.

Before any digging could be done, an area sixty feet wide, marked by red stakes on both sides, had to be cleared. Within this, forty feet would be excavated for the canal itself; the other twenty feet accounted for the towpath on one side, along which horses would tow the boats, and a berm so that people could move on the other side. Much of the canal route went through forests, dense with massive trees that had been undisturbed for generations. The work of removing these trees was called "grubbing standing timber," and early on, even one tree required several men and more than a hundred swings of an ax. Then, someone came up with a way that one man could take down many trees with a fraction of the exertion.

According to this new technique, a chain was tied high in a tree with the other end leading to a wheel worked by an endless-screw gear. As a man wound the gear with a crank, the tree was very slowly pulled over with irresistible force. This not only pulled down the tree, but yanked out the roots as well.

Stumps still in the earth from previously cleared land remained a problem until someone came up with a stump-pulling device that was as effective as it was simple. It had two tremendous wheels, sixteen feet in diameter, on the ends of a very sturdy axle thirty feet long. Fixed at the center of the axle was a slightly smaller wheel, fourteen feet in diameter, with a broad rim that held a coiled rope. This strange-looking machine was hauled into place so it straddled the stump, and the big outer wheels were tied down to hold it steady. A chain wound around the axle was tied to the stump, and a team of horses was hitched to the end of a rope that was wound around the rim of the middle wheel. Then as the animals strained, the rope grew taut, and made the center wheel rotate. This moved the axle which, in turn, wound up the chain that was fastened to the stump. The difference in size of wheel and axle multiplied the force tremendously, and the stump came out of the ground with a snapping and popping of roots as neatly as could be. Seven men and two horses could pull thirty to forty stumps in one day with this rig.

The men who devised these methods were not the engineers, nor were they scientists or inventors. They were the laborers – the hired hands doing the heavy lifting on the line – whom history does not remember by name. They did not seek credit and so their accomplishments, when recorded in the engineers' reports, remained anonymous. At celebrations heralding the opening of each section of the canal, these men were only faces in the crowd. But without them, the Erie Canal might never have been completed.

In such ingenious ways, the problems of making a canal were met and conquered - and the rate of progress improved steadily.

Once the land was cleared, the excavation began. The workers dug with shovels, spades, and pickaxes, and carted off the dirt in wheelbarrows. Some saved both time and effort by using horse-drawn plows, which easily cut through the earth and roots with blades of sharpened iron. Horses could also carry off larger loads of the loose earth, while their hooves tamped down the sides of the canal into solid banks that would be less vulnerable to leaks.

No amount of Yankee ingenuity could surmount the weather. During the first winter, 1818-19, work on the canal was stopped due to unusually heavy snowfall. Snow drifts six feet deep blocked roads needed to haul materials and supplies. It was late May before snow began to melt; and this runoff, combined with heavy rains, caused more problems. Crews had to wait for the mud and puddles to dry out before work could resume. But these problems were minor compared to what the heat would bring.

Most of the time lost because of the snow was made up by the vigorous efforts of nearly 4,000 men and 1,500 horses that spring of 1819. Frequently on hand to see that things kept moving was De Witt Clinton, who tried to get away from his duties as governor as often as possible to ride a horse or stagecoach up and down the canal route. Canal commissioners could also often be found at the worksites. Myron Holley, a New York State assemblyman from Ontario County, named to the Erie Canal Commission in 1816, rode in a carriage to dole out money to contractors so they could pay the workers.

The progress was encouraging, leading Clinton to boast that his promise to have the Big Ditch finished in 1823 still held.

"The completion of these stupendous works will spread the blessings of plenty and opulence [to] the most distant parts of the Union and command the approbation of the civilized world," he said. At least in part, Clinton's timeline was tied to his political aspirations: He would be up for re-election as governor of New York in 1820; four years later, at the end of President James Monroe's likely second term, the presidential race would be wide open. But his enemies guffawed, and even his friends urged him not to make such rash statements.

At one point, it looked as though the canal was going to be stopped dead long before 1823. The middle section had been selected largely because it seemed to be the easiest digging, but one part of it turned out to be a nightmare.

Another bad winter, which seemed to be one endless blizzard, left the ground everywhere muddy and soft. The worst of it was near the west end, at the outlet of Cayuga Lake, where a low, marshy area crossed the line of the canal for four-and-a-half miles. The Montezuma Marshes, named after a small village on their edge, were a dismal spot with impenetrable thickets of rushes taller than a man, and oozy black muck underfoot.

In the spring, rain caused the Seneca River nearby to spill over its banks and drain into the marshes. This delayed work on the canal for three weeks, from May to June 1820, during which the men sat in their bunkhouses waiting for the river level to go down. Cayuga Indians, some of whom were hired on to the canal project, had warned the surveyors about the problems of working in the marshes – particularly the mosquitoes. Many of the local laborers were also reluctant to work in this area. But these warnings were largely ignored.

The first day in the marshes, the men joked about the easy digging. But the next morning, the soft mud they had shoveled out had settled and flowed back into the ditch. There was little sign of the channel dug the day before. So, to keep the sides of the canal firm, they constructed retaining walls of planks, held in place by long stakes driven down through the soft mud and into the firm layer of clay beneath. That worked fairly well, except that occasionally a man would pound a stake through the mire into the clay only to watch it sink into bottomless quicksand. About one in twenty stakes was lost this way.

Even the Irishmen, who had shown a knack for working in swampy places, did not like this spot. Because of the heat, the laborers all worked shirtless and suffered sunburns. Their legs swelled from standing in the water for hours, and leeches fastened onto them. But they kept their sense of humor, giving such names to the worst places as "Bottomless Pit," "Digger's Misery," "Back break Bog," and "Mudturtles' Delight." They also added to their song:

> We are digging the Ditch through the mire;
> Through the mud and the slime and the mire, by heck!
> And the mud is our principal hire;
> In our pants, up our sleeves, down our neck, by heck!
> The mud is our principal hire.

But mosquitoes, arriving in large swarms by the middle of July, were the worst of the canal diggers' miseries. Enormous clouds of the insects fell on the men in such savage numbers that their hands swelled until they could hardly hold their tools, and their eyes were puffed almost shut. The men were supplied with little smudge pots – each containing a small glowing fire covered with green leaves to create dense smoke – which they wore around their necks to ward off the mosquitoes. They called them "Montezuma necklaces." The smoke helped somewhat with the mosquito problem, but had its own side effects: raw noses, red eyes, and terrible coughing fits.

One of the pests making life so miserable was the anopheles mosquito, the carrier of malaria - although no one yet connected the insect with the disease. By early August, hundreds of workers were coming down with chills and fevers. Believing bad air was the cause ("malaria" is an Italian word, meaning "bad air"), many able men walked off the job to get clear of it. Others were too weak, and shaking, to even get up out of their bunks for breakfast. A traveler passing through found a doctor working himself hollow-eyed, caring for throngs of patients night and day. His first treatments - bleeding, and the administration of feverwort, snakeroot, green pigweed, and Seneca Oil (known as petroleum in later years) - had done little for the men. He also tried a new drug from Peru called "Jesuit's Bark," which seemed to do some good. In fact, the bark contained quinine – later recognized as the best treatment for malaria. Still, more than 1,000 workers died.

Soon, work in the Montezuma Marshes stopped completely, and there was dark talk about giving up the whole project. Contractors scrambled to hire replacement workers. A New York newspaper on August 15 carried this notice: "Two hundred men wanted at once for the Cayuga Marshes. No wet feet. No disease. Top Pay." Another posted at the

Exchange Hotel in Auburn read: "Wanted men . . . Pleasant work . . . Tavern-style keep . . . High wages." But even promises of $1 a day, and "whiskey every night if you get the shakes," were not enough to coax men who had heard about the horrors of the marshes.

When autumn came, the sickness disappeared with the mosquitoes - and the work went ahead once again. Now there was determination to finish before another summer brought back the heat and mosquitoes. Contractors advertised for: "FIVE HUNDRED LABORERS . . . wanted for about ten weeks to work in the construction of the Canal through the Cayuga Marshes. Good hands shall receive from twelve to thirteen dollars per month, week, or day, at their option. They shall be well fed, and lodged in comfortable shanties, with sufficient blankets. They will be subject to some inconvenience, from water and mud; but a portion of the work will be dry; and all experience proves that men may labor on the Marsh without any unusual exposure of health until the middle of July, before which it is intended to have this portion of the Canal completed. . . ."

Under the weight of this added pressure, the feats of workers on the middle canal are extraordinary. One of the bridges across the marshes was a marvel of the Big Ditch. It was a wooden structure built on stone piles which spanned some 1,300 feet of marshy ground. The bridge was part of the towpath, and provided solid ground for the horses and tow teams.

Work on one vital and extensive part of the canal - the feeder system which supplied the canal with water - went on almost unknown, because it was done miles from the

Erie itself. The slightly downward slope of the canal, which dropped from Lake Erie to the Hudson River, created a very gentle eastward flow of its water. This flow, together with continual evaporation and leakage of the canal's water, meant it had to be replenished all along the way. And so, while the Big Ditch itself was being dug, there was construction on a complex system of feeder channels and dammed streams to utilize the resources of all the nearby rivers and creeks.

This system would bring water to the Erie under the control of sluice gates and waste gates, which regulated the flow into the canal. Some of the feeder channels had a double purpose; they were to carry boats, and in time formed a small system of branch canals which opened up trade with farms and settlements hundreds of miles away from the centers of commerce.

Fifteen Miles on the Erie Canal

Despite all problems and distractions, the middle section of the Erie Canal was about 95 percent complete by late summer 1819. A vote of authorization by the New York State Legislature on April 7, 1819, meant that work could soon begin on the east and west sections. The state budget was operating at a surplus, and investments in the Canal Fund were ample enough that the legislature also agreed to suspend a tax on lands adjacent to the canal, which had been enacted but never collected. And to speed up the project, a law was passed exempting canal workers from militia service, addressing commissioners' concerns that frequent call-ups were disruptive. That autumn, the time had come for a celebration.

On October 21, 1819, a little more than two years after the first groundbreaking ceremony at Rome, another crowd gathered there to celebrate the opening of the first stretch of canal. It was not much of a channel, extending only fifteen miles between Rome and Utica. But the commissioners had decided it was important to call attention to the progress that had been made. People wanted a canal, but when it was not dug overnight, they became impatient. Clinton, who had been swept into the governor's office so overwhelmingly two years before, had become very unpopular by 1819. A piece of finished canal might convince the people that the Erie was coming right along, and that Clinton and the other commissioners had been on the job.

Shortly after sunrise, the sluice gates were opened, and water rushed into the channel from the west. Elkahan Watson, the world traveler who more than thirty years before had envisioned this moment, described the scene as "truly sublime. . . . It was impossible for stupidity itself not to have been electrified on this joyous occasion, and to stretch their opaque minds from Erie to the ocean." The event was celebrated with the usual speechmaking, firing of cannons, and hurrahing. One local observer told the *Albany Gazette:* "The waters were rushing in from the westward and coming down their untried channel toward the sea. . . . As this new internal river rolled its first waves through the state . . . the people were running across the fields, climbing on trees and fences, and crowding the bank of the canal to gaze upon the welcome sight."

Then a new boat, named the *Chief Engineer of Rome* to compliment Chief Engineer Benjamin Wright, became the first to float on Erie water. Sixty-one-feet long, seven and a half feet wide, and light enough to draw only fourteen inches of water, the boat was towed by a pair of sturdy horses from Rome to Utica in one day, and back the next. On board were Governor De Witt Clinton and thirty of his guests – including the canal commissioners, the engineers, other state dignitaries, and a small military band that played music to the delight of people lined up along the route. Others climbed aboard along the way, until the passengers numbered at least seventy.

At every town and village they passed, there were exuberant public demonstrations. Hundreds of cheering spectators followed the boat. At Whitesboro, a short distance from Utica, the local militia fired a twenty-one gun salute. Church bells rang and drums rolled as the passengers unloaded at Utica, and transferred to carriages that delivered them and their luggage to Bagg's Hotel. At exactly 9:15 the next morning, they were headed back down the canal to Rome. The entire thirty-mile round trip, according to one newspaper report, took only eight hours and twenty minutes – four miles an hour was considered a sensational speed, and would become standard for boats on the canal.

Not everyone was excited. Enemies of the governor and the canal sneered, saying that at the rate of fifteen miles every two years, it would take forever to build the Erie.

But considerably more than that had been done. Just about all the ninety-four miles of the middle section had been cleared - forty-eight of which had been dug - and another eight-mile length was ready for travel as soon as it passed inspection. Things were progressing steadily on the Erie Canal.

That first fifteen-mile stretch immediately began to play an important part in the great westward migration. And for the people living beside it, it became a new and fascinating plaything.

Almost every canal-side dweller built himself a boat to float on the Erie. Most were carelessly built and leaked badly; as often as not, they settled to the bottom where the owner let them rest. Farmers found the channel convenient for floating logs from one part of their farms to another, but they had the bad habit of leaving the logs in the channel for several days until they got around to hauling them out. The canal also developed into a fine place for fishing. The towpath was used for a road, and some of the more sporting-minded farmers even used it as a race track. At times, the path was so cluttered with straying barnyard animals that a team towing a canal boat on honest business had a hard time getting through. Finally, a fence was built to keep the wandering animals off the towpath.

The canal boat captains complained bitterly about all this sort of activity. More than one canal boat had sprung a leak after smashing against the sunken arks abandoned by "backwoods bumpkins playing canal men." The commissioners did set up a system of fines — $5 for throwing rubbish into the channel, $10 for leaving a sunken boat, etc. - but it was not strictly enforced. The commissioners did not want to make enemies of the country folk at a time when the canal needed every possible friend.

The same boat captains who demanded strict controls on outside canal use had a different view of the tolls that were put into effect beginning on July 1, 1820. Boats hauling merchandise were taxed at two cents a ton per mile, and half that for farming supplies and equipment; no toll was yet levied on passengers. Scales were erected at stations to weigh the boats. Some captains muffled the feet of their horses by wrapping them in cloths and tried to sneak by the toll stations at night without paying. The fine for breaching toll regulations could be as high as $25, assuming the offender was caught. The toll collector at Rome made a network of iron chains that he could lower into the water with a winch when night fell. After he caught a few boats trying to slip by his station, the practice of toll-dodging on the first small length of the Erie Canal came to an end.

These problems paled to what had been achieved by dogged determination, and men with shovels, pickaxes, plows, and pulleys. As the canal commissioners, in their 1820 report to the New York State Legislature, eloquently put it: "The novelty of seeing large boats drawn by horses, upon waters . . . through cultivated fields, forests, swamps, over ravines, creeks and morasses, and from one elevation to another, by means of ample beautiful and substantial locks, has been eminently exhilerating. The precision of the levels, the solidity of the banks, the regularity of the curves, the symmetry of the numerous and massive stone works, the depth of the excavation in some places, the extent of the embankments in others, and the impression produced everywhere along the line, by the visible effects of immense labor, have uniformly afforded gratification mingled with surprise."

3

CLINTON'S TRIUMPH

Governor De Witt Clinton's enemies scoffed when the first fifteen-mile stretch of canal was opened: Fifteen miles out of 363; now wasn't that something to boast about! Fifteen miles in two years! "Clinton's Ditch," they said, was a mad project that would never be finished. It was sure to run the state far into debt if it was not stopped.

"Clinton's Ditch" later would be used with affection, but midway through the building of the canal, it was a taunt. Troubles were piling up: Towns which the canal bypassed were lobbying for a change of route; construction was moving much slower than most people had expected; no revenues had come in yet from the opened stretches of canal. Nothing seemed to go smoothly for Clinton, even though he soon gave the state plenty of canal.

The governor had been beset by personal turmoil, too. During the summer of 1818, as canal workers in the Montezuma marshes were dying from malaria, Clinton's wife of twenty-two years, Maria, had also become gravely ill. The Clintons fled the swarms of mosquitoes at their Staten Island home, but encountered more at Mount Vernon, in Winchester County. Maria died on July 30, 1818, at age forty-two. Shortly after, Clinton suffered a terrible fall from his horse, which left him with a bad limp the rest of his life. But, not one to stay down, he remarried in 1819 – his new wife was Catherine Jones, the daughter of a New York physician – and quickly got back on his horse, riding it up and down the canal route to check its progress.

The year 1819 had brought nothing but misery to most Americans. The "Era of Good Feelings," which had swept the nation after the War of 1812, had ended in the United

States' first major peacetime financial crisis. The Panic of 1819 was triggered, in large part, by a bill that had come due on the Louisiana Purchase of 1803, forcing the U.S. government to pay France $3 million in gold that it didn't have. This led to curtailment of federal loans, foreclosure of heavily mortgaged farms, widespread bankruptcies, and mass unemployment – from which the nation would not begin to recover until 1821. But the depression was actually a boon to the Erie Canal.

At a time when most companies were laying off workers, the Erie was hiring. Unemployed people flocked to New York, where more than 9,000 were hired onto the canal project. Investors, too, were easier to come by. At first considered high risk, Erie Canal bonds were now seen as a port in a storm - one of the few smart investments in the troubled economy. Before 1819, these subscriptions had been bought up mostly by small investors – with fifty-one of sixty-nine investing less than $2,000 in 1818. But now wealthy businessmen were buying up the bonds in multiples of $10,000. (By 1822, fur trader John Jacob Astor – American's first multi-millionaire – owned $213,000 in canal bonds.) Because of falling interest rates, borrowing costs also were lower. Of all the troubles that De Witt Clinton faced in building the canal, finding money was not one.

Any who needed to be convinced of the project's merits might be treated to a boat ride on the canal. The *Cayuga Republican* newspaper of Auburn reported on one such ride, organized by canal commissioner Myron Holley, on December 9, 1819. Holley took investors along on a test ride of the canal from the marshes at Montezuma to the village of Jordan. Despite being towed by two horses through ice as thick as two inches, a sixty-foot boat traveled sixteen miles in about six hours. The test was a success, with one passenger noting that the trip was "comfortable and pleasant" despite the "inclement season."

The next year, 1820, water was admitted from the reserve basins into one part after another of the Erie. On April 20, a canal boat named *Montezuma* for the community where it was built, arrived at Syracuse, and about 100 people went aboard for a mile and a half ride. As one witness described:

> This was the first great event in that place. It had been extensively advertised, and nearly every inhabitant for many miles around had gathered on the banks of the canal, anxious to see the great site. . . . from the first, there were many who believed the scheme was not practicable, and this faction was well represented in the assembled crowd, and many who had been standing expectantly for hours became tired and joined the doubters, who were shouting that "tomorrow you will hear that the *Montezuma* bumped her nose against the bank, and sunk before she had floated a mile, and we wish old Clinton had gone down with her,
>
> and sunk in the ditch he has made at our expense."
>
> While all this was going on, at once, there was a shout of "There she comes! She is coming!" . . . as they passed the crowd of spectators, the horses were on a fast trot, a wave of

water was forced wide over the low banks,
and a loud shout arose from the crowd. This
successful trip silenced all doubters and the
canal was acknowledged to be a success.

Anticipation was building for another big event. On the
Fourth of July, seventy-three fine new canal boats left Syracuse in a parade, as speeches were made and fireworks filled
the sky to mark the completion of nearly all of the canal's
middle section. The celebration had barely ended before the
same boats were at work hauling produce, merchandise, and
travelers along the newly opened canal route. By virtue of
being on the canal route, Syracuse – a community of barely
250 people in 1820 – would grow to a city with a population
of more than 22,000 by 1850.

But even this progress did not revive Governor De Witt
Clinton's fading popularity. The tide of public opinion was
running too strongly against him. On Election Day in 1820,
he barely retained his office, polling only 2,000 more votes
than Daniel Tompkins, the former governor and sitting Vice
President of the United States, who had tried to unseat him.

Along with this setback, Clinton had to announce that he
could not meet his campaign promise to have the canal
finished by 1823. Difficulties had arisen, he said, and progress had been slower than expected. But he promised that it
definitely would be ready for business by 1825. Once again,
there was an uproar from his rivals, who said that the Ditch
would not be finished in 1825 or any other year.

The criticism, however, did not stop the governor. He was
much too busy pushing his crews to even consider failure.
Except for the crossing of the Montezuma Marshes, the

middle section had presented no other major engineering problems. But the builders faced one tough problem after another as they went to work on the eastern and western sections. Much of the land was rough and hilly, with deep valleys crossing the canal route, and lots of rock to be blasted out. And almost all of the canal's eighty-three locks still had to be built to compensate for the long rise from the Hudson River to Lake Erie.

Locks and Aqueducts

Where the route of a canal runs along level ground, construction can proceed smoothly. If a river crosses its course, the engineering need not be too difficult. In some cases, a bridge for the towpath can easily be built, and the canal boats towed across the river. In other cases, particularly where a river's water is seasonally higher or lower than the canal, simple guard locks can be built to keep the river from flooding or clogging the canal. Hilly country, however, is consistently troublesome for canal builders.

And it was hilly country that Clinton's engineers began cutting through in 1820. Streams that lay in the way were usually in deep valleys much lower than the canal. The only way to get the waterway across was to put it on an aqueduct. They also had to build about 300 small bridges - a few for country roads that the canal cut across, but most for farmers whose lands had been split by the waterway. The state of New York had promised that it would build "occupation bridges" (so called because they allowed the owners to continue their occupation of farming) wherever their land was cut. To save money, the bridges were made low - only seven and a half feet above the water.

Many of the aqueducts were amazing works for their time. Most were of stone-arch construction, but others consisted of stone piers supporting trough-like wooden structures which carried the canal across the valley. The men surveying the lower Mohawk River for level terrain were forced to shift the route of the waterway back and forth across the river several times.

Two of the aqueducts that carried the Erie on these crossings were architectural marvels. The one below Schenectady, at Cohoes Falls, was probably the most famous: The longest of eighteen aqueducts on the canal, it stretched across twenty-six stone piers for 1,188 feet. The other aqueduct, at Little Falls, was 744 feet long and spanned the river with three huge stone arches thirty feet high.

Many of the aqueducts along the Erie had special claims to fame because of height or ingenuity of construction. The one at Rochester was the longest stone-arch bridge in the world when built: It was 802 feet long and had nine Roman arches which stretched fifty feet above the turbulent Genesee River.

To build the Genesee aqueduct, the canal engineers hired William Britton, who had just completed another project for the state of New York: a prison. The prison in Auburn was surrounded by formidable walls, twenty feet high, to keep the inmates in. But Britton had thirty convicts assigned to him for the aqueduct project. He provided lodging, on an island between the river and a grist mill on the west side, but paid no wages and kept the convicts tethered with ball and chain. Still, the convicts spent as much time trying to escape as they did blasting and cutting rock along the riverbanks into blocks for the aqueduct. Seven of them, probably good swimmers, did escape. More convicts were obtained from the prison as replacements; but now guards were needed, too, and this labor was not free.

There were more problems for the aqueduct during the winter of 1821, when the ice-choked Genesee River spilled its banks and carried away the foundations for one of the piers. That same December, William Britton died; the rumor was suicide. A new contract was signed, with Alfred Hovey, who had overseen the canal building through the Montezuma marshes. Work started up again the next spring, this time with the local farmers and Irish immigrants.

The rock that Britton's convicts had removed – mostly gray limestone and reddish-brown sandstone – left the riverbed uneven, and now little of the foundation remained. A new source of sandstone was discovered at a quarry near the town of Greece, about fifteen miles east of Rochester. Workers cut huge blocks of the sandstone and shipped it down a short, lateral canal they had dug to connect with the Erie. On the western ridge of the Genesee valley, they built a large, rugged wooden chute, which they used to slide the blocks into place.

Finally completed, eleven months behind schedule in September 1823, the Rochester aqueduct cost $83,000 more than had been projected. It was considered a miracle of engineering – able to support 2,000 gallons of canal water, and to convey boats through an area that before was only dark wilderness. The usual reverie marked its dedication on October 6, when a procession of decorated boats, barges, and rafts floated proudly across the aqueduct. Workmen, eager to spend their hard-earned wages, enjoyed a lavish feast at a Rochester tavern, where they raised their glasses of beer in at least twenty-five different toasts.

Shortly after the festivities, the first commercial boat across the aqueduct carried flour from Little Falls. In the first ten days of operation, about 10,000 barrels of flour went east through Rochester, which soon would become known as the nation's Flour City. Other goods, of course, were transported. One popular story was told about a shipment of oysters, which arrived in Rochester still fresh after traveling more than 400 miles from the Atlantic Ocean. The speed of commerce was staggering. De Witt Clinton called the aqueduct "a sublime work," which made Rochester into "a growing place . . . [with] the hum of men . . . the bustle of business . . . and streets crowded with building stone."

But this noble structure leaked badly, though limestone had been used in places to help fortify the red sandstone. Also, its channel was so narrow - only seventeen feet wide - that boats could not pass each other on it. Many legendary battles broke out between crews of canal boats, which had entered from opposite sides at about the same time and claimed the right of way when they met in the middle. These fights, according to a prominent Rochester citizen and lawyer named Frederick A. Whittlesey, were an almost daily occurrence. "Long detentions on this account were not infrequent," he wrote, "and as there was no railing on the berm bank a contest became serious." Finally, to enter and exit the aqueduct, boats had to make a right-angle turn – the tightest bend on the entire Erie Canal. If two barges were lashed together, they were forced to separate to complete the maneuver. All of these problems combined to compel the construction of a replacement aqueduct, ten years after the first, which was wider and did not leak.

Each project revealed more and more challenges. While work was still underway on the Genesee River, crews east of Rochester were faced with another deep chasm. Cutting across the canal route where the Irondequoit Creek runs north to Lake Ontario, the distance from one edge of the gap to the other was about a mile – too narrow for locks to be built. Engineers also abandoned plans to build a wooden aqueduct, as tall as a six-story building, which they thought might easily be toppled by the strong winds blowing in from Lake Ontario. That left one option: Filling the valley.

To avoid blocking the Irondequoit, a stone culvert – twenty-five feet high, thirty feet wide, and 100 feet long – had to be built at the bottom. Care was taken in the construction of the stone arches, so that they could support the weight of more than forty feet of earth as well as the canal running across the embankment. The soil presented another problem: On both sides of the creek, there was mostly loose quicksand, which could easily wash away and carry the canal with it. The engineers' solution was to sink more than 900 twenty-foot log pilings into the quicksand; then firmer dirt was brought in to fill the area above the culvert.

About 3,000 Irishmen worked on the Irondequoit embankment, supervised by J.J. McShane, the lead contractor. McShane was a big, brawny man - a former prizefighter from the town of Tipperary, Ireland - but unlike most contractors on the Erie, he had experience building canals in Ireland. A tough taskmaster, he worked the men day and night, by bonfire or torchlight. But he paid a fair wage – seventy-five cents a day – and provided a "jigger boss," a man who went along the line dispensing whiskey to the workers several times throughout the day.

It was back-breaking work: Every bit of dirt had to be dug up with picks and shovels from nearby fields and hills, and hauled by wheelbarrows and horse-drawn carts to the valley. The wheelbarrow men were led by a "pacer," with whom they had to struggle to keep up. Building up the embankment took most of two years - not pausing even during the hottest months of summer or the heaviest snowfalls of winter - and was complete by October 1822. But still, the work was not done.

Next, a canal trough was cut along the top, and built with heavy square timbers. McShane worried about how to make it hold water until, one day, a farmer showed him a deposit of blue clay. A layer of the blue clay three inches thick was laid over the timbers and allowed to harden for seven days before the first foot of water was let in. After two days of observation, the water level was raised another foot. The tests were successful; there was no leaking. Now it was the spring of 1823, and a great rainstorm came to fill up the canal. Believing the rain was divine providence, McShane declared the embankment open to navigation, but limited to boats with a draft of not more than twenty inches. One of the first boats to cross it carried eight families – sixty people in all, each of whom paid $1.50 for the ride from Utica to Rochester. The blue clay held up well enough at first to the traffic; later, it would be replaced with stone and concrete.

There was another grave problem in the east at Little Falls, where the old Western Inland Lock Navigation Company had once done so much for travel on the Mohawk River. The earlier builders had constructed locks to take the river traffic around the falls - and had spent several years doing it. The Erie Canal planners, however, brought their waterway up the opposite side of the river - ignoring the battered old locks and channel. They asked William Weston, the famous English canal engineer, for an opinion on how long it would take to hack a new channel through the solid rock and to build a set of locks. He looked over the situation, checked the plans, inspected the rock, and made a number of calculations. "Two years," he said. They thanked him and paid his fee. Then they brought in their own crack crews and hired some hard-rock miners to teach them how to use explosives. In less than three months, the channel was dug, although it took somewhat longer to finish the locks.

Very often now, they were working in rock, and the laborers had added still another verse to their song about building the Big Ditch:

> We are cutting the Ditch through the rocks,
> Through the rocks across the state, by heck!
> We are cutting the Ditch through the rocks,
> And we'll finish her off with stone locks,
> From the rocks across the state, by heck!
> From the rocks across the state.

Here again, Yankee ingenuity came into play. One method involved drilling rows of holes into the stone, and filling the holes with black gunpowder, which when ignited blasted loose blocks two feet wide and a foot and a half deep.

Another method relied on nature. Eight-inch-deep holes drilled a foot apart were filled with water in the winter. As temperatures dropped below freezing, sharp cracks – like gunshots – could be heard as the expanding ice created fissures in the stone. Wedges then driven into these cracks easily broke off large blocks.

The new tricks of rock cutting and aqueduct building were nothing compared to what the engineers and crews had to learn about building locks. Fifty-three locks had to be constructed in the 100-mile stretch between Albany and Schenectady. The sixteen miles between Troy and Schenectady – over which the land dropped more than 200 feet - accounted for twenty-seven locks, nearly a third of all locks on the Erie Canal. Here, the cost per mile more than doubled; the total expense of the Albany-Schenectady route was $540,000. Commissioners admitted that if the canal project had started with this section, it would have been aborted and postponed for as long as 100 years.

Far to the west, the engineers were working at the biggest problem of all: How to get the canal up the steep rock face at Lockport - a town near the Niagara Falls that would get its name from its famous system of locks. Before the work had begun, it had been home to only three families. After contracts were signed in January 1823, it grew to 337 families. By the time the job was completed, two and a half years later, there would be a population of about 3,000 – not counting the nearly 2,000 laborers, who were mostly Irish immigrants.

At Lockport, north of Buffalo, the rocky land rose sharply to the level almost of a cliff. Nathan S. Roberts, one of the

Erie's self-made engineers, had pondered long about how he was going to get the canal up that rock face. With no one to help him, and no guidance except a few books, he designed a double set of five locks. This was the only place on the Erie where there were two sets of locks - one set for eastbound and another for westbound travel. They were needed to avoid hopeless bottlenecks; otherwise, a boat going one way would have had to pass through all five locks before a boat coming the other way could start through.

These were "flights of locks," rising one after another like a giant staircase for a six-story building. Each lock had a lift of twelve feet instead of the usual eight feet four inches, and were cut out of solid rock - even the towpath. At one point on their shelf-like path, horses and driver were a dizzy sixty feet above the lock. The "Deep Cut" stopped about thirteen feet below the highest peak, creating a channel right through the rock face, and eliminating the need for a sixth set of locks.

The cut presented its own challenges, of course. Many steel drill bits were broken trying to punch holes in the rock, until someone came up with a method of tempering and hardening the steel. The holes were filled with gunpowder, and an explosion sheared off large blocks. But this also sent huge chunks of rock flying, and sometimes raining down on the town of Lockport. Often, the fuse was lit by a schoolboy from the town who, it was decided, could run to safety faster than a grown man. To remove debris piling up in the bottom of the cut, a system of derricks was devised in which horses pulled cables that lifted out large buckets of the rock.

Crews finally broke through the last few feet of the Lockport peak in October 1824, and the amazing system of locks and canal were completed by June 1825. About 5,000 people attended the ceremonial opening, during which a bronze capstone memorial was placed at the foot of the locks that read: "Let posterity be excited to perpetuate our free institutions, and to make still greater efforts than our ancestors, to promote public prosperity, by the recollection that these works of internal improvements were achieved by the spirit and perseverance of REPUBLICAN FREE MEN."

The cutting on the western canal was not done. From Lockport west to Buffalo, a route had to be cut that was below the level of Lake Erie. By a gradual slope, dropping about an inch for every mile, the lake would become an inexhaustible water supply for the western end of the canal. A gentle flow of lake water would move continually along the twenty-five miles from Buffalo to Lockport, carrying boats laden with people and goods from west to east and back.

"Like An Old Brass Kettle"

In the meantime, De Witt Clinton might have been getting things done on the construction of the canal, but he was still having his troubles elsewhere. In 1822, the anti-canal factions combined against him were so strong that he did not receive the nomination for governor. New York's new governor was Joseph C. Yates, the former State Supreme Court justice, who on the Council of Revision had nearly succeeded in blocking the Erie Canal in 1817. Clinton had asserted that "if I had been a candidate, I would have been re-elected governor." But Yates's landslide victory – backed by 98 percent of voters – seemed to signal a shift in public sentiment regarding the Erie Canal.

Now, opposition was coming not only from politicians and crackpots, but many of the taxpayers as well. The costs of the canal were mounting frighteningly. Several millions of dollars had been spent, and some people were convinced that when the canal was finished, it would never pay for itself. Surely it would be better to drop it now, some believed, than to go on eternally paying its debts. These doubts, which arose from delays caused by the difficulties in digging the eastern and western sections of the canal, could only be cured by more progress and unequivocal results.

Still as canal commissioner, Clinton continued to push the project that had become the one absorbing interest of his life. Referring to this determination, a friend gave a toast, which Clinton preserved in his diary: "Like an old brass kettle . . . the harder he is rubbed, the brighter he will shine."

Aware that time was growing short, Clinton worked feverishly. He urged his men on, settled problems, and saw that equipment and materials were on hand when and where they were needed. Regularly, from time to time, sluice gates leading from reservoirs and feeder channels were opened to let water into still another length of canal. By midsummer of 1822, the Erie was carrying water all along the 280 miles of its projected route. And just before the fall freeze-up put an end to work that year, boats were also operating between Little Falls and Schenectady. Clinton's Ditch had become the biggest ditch anyone had ever seen.

But by then, Clinton's friends no longer made up the majority on the Erie Canal Commission. Through political maneuvering, the Tammany Hall faction of Democrats – called Bucktails after their insignia, which featured a deer's tail – had taken control. This shift started in 1818, when Joseph Ellicott resigned from the commission, citing poor health. Ellicott was a Quaker, surveyor, lawyer, politician, and one of the Erie Canal's strongest supporters. To replace him, Clinton nominated another friend, Ephraim Hart. But the Bucktails blocked Hart's appointment by presenting their own nominee, Henry Seymour, who won the New York Senate's confirmation by a margin of one vote.

In 1920, New York legislators passed the "Two Million Bill," which appropriated $1 million over the next two years to canal construction. Attached to the bill was a provision requiring one member to be added to the canal commission. Realizing that the Bucktails would use this to gain a majority on the commission, Governor Clinton was tempted to veto the bill. But either way, the Bucktails would win. If Clinton vetoed the bill, he risked losing needed state funds and further delaying the canal project; the Bucktails, meanwhile, could claim that they, not Clinton, were the true canal champions. Signing the bill assured that the canal would be completed, though the process would be more contentious with another Bucktail on the board. Clinton chose the latter.

Even after the Bucktails convened a constitutional convention to reduce his term as governor from four years to two years, Clinton expressed hope that "whatever diversity of opinion may exist . . . we will all cooperate . . . in cherishing a spirit of conciliation and forbearance, and in cultivating that respect which we owe to each other and to ourselves."

Then, on April 12, 1824, Clinton's political enemies - believing they were strong enough to move against the champion of the canal - stripped him of his one remaining office, the one that really counted. By a vote in the New York Senate of twenty-four to three, Clinton was removed from his position as a canal commissioner, an office he had held for fourteen years.

One of the three senators who voted no, Senator Henry Cunningham, spoke in Clinton's defense: "I hope there is yet a redeeming spirit in this house – that we will not be guilty of so great an outrage. . . . What, let me ask, shall we answer in excuse for ourselves, when we return to an inquisitive and watchful people? . . . What can we say [Clinton] has been guilty of, that he should be singled out as an object of state vengeance? . . . This resolution was engendered in the most unhallowed feelings of malice, to effect some nefarious secret purpose at the expense of the honor and integrity of this legislature." Though this had no immediate effect on the vote, Cunningham predicted that Clinton's legacy would be redeemed by history as "a proud monument . . . as imperishable as the splendid works which owe their origins to his genius and perseverance." In less time than the senator probably expected, his prediction proved correct.

For a frightening moment, it looked as though the anti-canal forces might be able to stop work entirely on the Erie. Hundreds of canal proposals before the state legislature suggested changing the course of the canal, or finishing only one section rather than all of the waterway, or stopping funds for locks.

But Clinton's political enemies had gone too far. Financial

reports, citing toll collections, proved that travelers were eagerly using what there was of the Erie, even though they had to haul their goods by wagon around the unopened sections. Some 1,822 boats were operating on one stretch only forty-five miles long, out beyond the growing wilderness village of Rochester. On this section alone, almost $21,000 in tolls had been collected in six months. By the end of the summer, the total collected by all operating sections of the canal was almost $300,000. Those who had opposed Clinton because they honestly believed the canal would always be a money-loser began to feel that the former governor had been treated unjustly. Now, they threw their support behind him.

Crowds gathered to protest Clinton's removal from the canal commission. Because no meeting hall in Albany or New York City was large enough to hold them all, more than 10,000 protesters swarmed City Hall Park, not far from Tammany Hall's headquarters, for their "indignation meeting." At his Albany home, Clinton was visited by twenty-five distinguished citizens, who informed him of the initiative to restore him to power. This group of supporters bought space in the April 20 *Albany Gazette* newspaper; the advertisement appeared as a Corinthian column, over which was written:

This MONUMENT is erected
for the eminent services
of that distinguished
benefactor of mankind
DE WITT CLINTON . . .
who has added imperishable
lustre on his own age,

and conferred innumerable
blessings on POSTERITY.

It was signed "FIAT JUSTICIA," meaning "LET JUSTICE
BE DONE."

The New York Senate refused to reverse its decision, and
Clinton did not return to the canal commission. But the
new wave of support did carry him to a nomination for
governor in the November 1824 election. His opponent was
Samuel Young, a Bucktail and canal commissioner. Because
of high interest in the canal – as well as a change in the
law that extended voting rights to all white males (not just
property owners) over the age of twenty-one – 190,545 New
Yorkers statewide (more than ever before) turned out to
vote. Clinton won by a comfortable majority of 103,452 to
87,093.

Soon after, in an election so close it had to be decided by
the House of Representatives, John Quincy Adams became
the sixth President of the United States. Adams promptly
moved to make DeWitt Clinton his Secretary of State, but
Clinton turned down the offer. In effect, as governor, Clinton again was in charge of the Erie Canal, and he felt obli-
gated to see the project through. Taking office on January
1, 1825, he announced that, in spite of the time he had lost,
the canal was still going to be ready by autumn - less than a
year away.

The remaining major projects were finished in good time.
The twenty-seven locks in the rocky climb from Albany
to Schenectady were completed, making it possible at last
to travel between the two cities by water. The western end
of the Erie Canal was the last section to be finished. A few

months after the completion of the five flights of locks at Lockport, water was admitted to the westernmost 140 miles of the canal.

Still, as Clinton's promised deadline approached, a few unfinished details remained to be addressed. The supervisors and crews hurried to take care of the most important ones. They built three weigh-locks at Troy, Utica, and Syracuse in which boats would be weighed to determine the amount of toll that they had to pay. Other, less vital matters were left until after the canal opened for business.

"Wedding of the Waters"

In October 1825, red and yellow leaves reflected in sparkling water from one end of the completed Erie Canal to the other. De Witt Clinton had kept his promise, and the state was delirious with happiness. On the splendid autumn morning of October 26, a great celebration got underway to hail the new canal and honor the man who had made it possible.

The festivities started in Buffalo. A parade, led by a brass band, escorted Governor Clinton and other dignitaries from the red-brick courthouse through the town to the canal. There they boarded the canal boat *Seneca Chief,* whose bright decorations included a huge oil painting of Clinton depicted as Hercules resting from his labors.

On the deck of the *Seneca Chief* were two kegs, decorated with eagles and in patriotic colors, both of which held water from Lake Erie. Later, in New York, they were to be poured into the ocean with a mixture of waters from the Mississippi, Columbia, Thames, La Plata, Seine, Rhine, Orinoco, Amazon, Nile, Gambia, Indus, and Ganges rivers in a "Wedding of the Waters."

Four other boats – the *Superior,* the *Commodore* Perry, the *Buffalo,* and a freight boat - followed the *Seneca Chief* in the official flotilla. Among the line of boats that came next was the *Noah's Ark,* which carried two Indian boys, a bear, two young deer, a beaver, two eagles, various other birds, and even a tank of fish - symbolizing the West before the coming of the white man. The *Niagara,* from Black Rock, brought up the rear. Its passengers included Peter Porter, who as a canal commissioner in 1816 had failed to route the Erie through Black Rock, and who the next year ran unsuccessfully against Clinton for governor. Today, he and the other critics were notably silent.

Jesse Hawley - a flour merchant from Geneva, New York, and an early and dedicated proponent of the canal – delivered a brief speech, in which he paid respects to the "projectors . . . statesmen . . . legislators . . . engineers . . . and men who had executed this magnificent work – an exhibition of the moral force of a free and enlightened people to the world."

At the boom of a cannon, the boats left Buffalo at 10:00 a.m. A few moments later, another cannoneer, several miles farther down the canal, heard the sound and fired his gun. In this way, the message was relayed all the way from Buffalo to New York City, 500 miles away. The last signal, fired at 11:20 a.m., triggered a tremendous artillery salute from New York. Then the line of gunners sent the same signal booming back, to let Buffalo know that New York had received the message.

Cadwallader D. Colden - a former New York City mayor and congressman, and grandson of the colonial governor who had dreamed about such a canal – remembered how he felt at the instant that the cannons were fired: "Who that has American blood in his veins can hear this sound without emotion? Who that has the privilege to do it can refrain from exclaiming, 'I too am an American citizen; and feel as much pride in being able to make the declaration, as ever an inhabitant of the eternal city felt in proclaiming he was a Roman.'"

The boats, each towed by a team of horses, had a quiet trip between towns because most of the country through which the canal ran was still wilderness. But at every town and hamlet, there was food and speechmaking. Many communities sent boats to join the official flotilla, which soon stretched far along the canal. At Rochester, the *Young Lion of the West* – which is how the locals described the town – carried two wolves, a fox, a fawn, four raccoons, and two eagles (all native creatures).

Canal towns had been preparing since midsummer for this event. Most of them had constructed what were called transparencies - boxes that had letters cut into their faces, with lanterns inside so their message could be read night or day. They were hung everywhere - on the sides of cabins, the signs were small, saying merely "CLINTON;" but others were huge, such as the one spanning the canal at Montezuma that proclaimed: "DE WITT CLINTON AND

INTERNAL IMPROVEMENTS." Fireworks were shot from the stone-arch aqueduct at Rochester. Tiny Bucksville, now Port Byron, could afford nothing so grand, but did its best by voting to keep every cabin in the village lighted until midnight.

Some of the towns along the canal, however, gave Clinton an icy reception. Rome, for instance, had grown into a thriving town on the canal built by the old Western Inland Lock Navigation Company. But the Erie had bypassed it by nearly half a mile, and prosperous businesses found themselves facing a stagnant ditch. Some of the unhappy citizens held their own "Wedding of the Waters" before Clinton and his fleet arrived. In a funeral-like procession, the townspeople carried a barrel of water from the old canal and dumped it into the Erie.

Schenectady was equally cold. The town had become prosperous by hauling people and freight from the Hudson River to Mohawk River boats. The Erie Canal might be good for the country, but it had ruined Schenectady's specialized business, and so the townspeople completely ignored Clinton's arrival. Only the students of Schenectady's Union College, who were young and optimistic about the canal, turned out to celebrate the governor and his party.

On November 2, after a trip of about a week, the *Seneca Chief* and her large following passed from the Erie Canal into the Hudson River. A twenty-four cannon salute sounded as Clinton and his party entered the canal's last lock at Albany. Cheering spectators crowded the shore, wharves, bridges, and their own boats which were lined up in the bay. "It was not a monarch which they hailed," recorded the

Albany Daily Advertiser, "but it was the majesty of genius supported by a free people that rode in triumph and commanded the admiration of men stout of heart and firm of purpose."

The celebration at Albany went all night. A parade escorted Clinton and the other dignitaries to the Assembly Hall, where a choir and full orchestra played between speeches. But the grandest display was later, on a bridge over the Hudson that had the look of a gothic cathedral, with its fourteen-foot-high pointed arches and gilded turrets. A massive tent stretched over tables with seating for 600 guests, who were treated to a feast, wines from the best vineyards of Europe, and an elaborate theatrical performance.

At 10:00 a.m. the next morning, the boats headed down the Hudson toward New York City. There, because there were no towpaths, a line of seven steamboats – each brightly decorated with streamers, and carrying a brass band – pulled the fleet into the harbor.

Governor Clinton was met by cannon salutes from the city's forts, by city dignitaries, and by swarms of boats with tooting whistles and cheering passengers. The *Seneca Chief* was towed out to Sandy Hook, where the New York harbor joins the Atlantic, and the ceremony of the "Wedding of the Waters" was carried out. Turning to his companions, Clinton declared: "The solemnity, at this place, on the first arrival of vessels from Lake Erie, is intended to indicate and commemorate the navigable communication, which has been accomplished between our Mediterranean Seas and the Atlantic Ocean, in about eight years, to the extent of more than four hundred and twenty-five miles, by the wisdom, public spirit, and energy of the people of the state of New York; and may God of the Heavens and the Earth smile most propitiously on the work, and render it subservient to the best interests of the human race."

The canal champion poured the two kegs of Lake Erie water into the ocean as a symbol that the Great Lakes and the Atlantic were now united. Then the mixture of river waters was emptied as a sign that commerce from all parts of the world could now be carried to the American West. Before the brief ceremony had ended, Clinton's face was wet with tears of emotion; he had worked so hard and suffered so much disappointment, and now, at last, the canal was truly finished.

New York City that day saw one of the greatest celebrations in its history. A parade, which is said to have been five miles long, reached the Battery just in time to welcome Clinton as he stepped ashore. Merchants hawked commemorative hats and handkerchiefs adorned with Clinton's likeness. There were spectacular fireworks, and signs everywhere hailed Clinton and the canal. During the evening, crowds walked by City Hall to admire the fairyland sight of a building lit by thousands of candles. Among the dignitaries in New York for the festivities were President John Quincy Adams; former Presidents John Adams, Thomas Jefferson, James Madison, and James Monroe; as well as the hotheaded politician Andrew Jackson.

Meanwhile, in the New England states, families held their own quiet, little celebrations. Now with smooth water all the way and no need to hire expensive wagon transport, the long journey to the western lands became much easier and cheaper. In New Hampshire and Connecticut, Massachusetts and Vermont, families packed the farm wagons that would carry them on the first leg of the trip. They took a final look at the house and barn and fields that were being abandoned to wind and rain and time - with so many people leaving, no one was buying farms. Then they turned away from the old home and did not look back again. From that moment, everything lay ahead, with the Erie Canal a shining ribbon leading to a new land and a new life.

4

TRAVEL ON THE ERIE

From the moment the Erie Canal opened, its waters were thronged with lines of vessels moving in opposite directions. The press of traffic was so great, particularly during the autumn and spring seasons, that boats often had to wait for hours before they could get through the locks. The Erie was too small for the amount of business it carried the very day that De Witt Clinton's triumph was proclaimed. Still, the journey from Albany to Buffalo – which in 1810 had taken De Witt Clinton and his fellow commissioners thirty-two days – now could be completed in no more than six days.

The nation had never seen anything like it. The major east-west transport of goods and people moved along the Erie, and each year the traffic increased. There was a constant bustle of emigrants going west to find new homes; of European visitors coming to see the sights they had read about; of politicians, merchants, army officers, and cattle traders; of clergymen trying to save souls, and gamblers busily separating careless travelers from their money. Cargo boats moving toward Lake Erie carried clocks, guns, needles, knives, whalebone corsets, bolts of cloth, and a thousand other articles the West wanted. Boats from the West carried the produce of farm and forest to the cities of the East Coast: potatoes, apples, cider, wheat and milled flour, whiskey, live turkeys, lumber, and precious furs.

Life was exciting for the people who traveled on Erie water, or worked on the canal, or lived beside it. Canal towns grew as fast as houses, with mills and stores being built by overworked carpenters and masons. Even the smallest hamlets shared in the excitement of the canal, as Erie businessman put up canal-side grocery stores, grogshops, and livery stables. But even for folks who just watched the boats go by, the Big Ditch always provided something of interest.

In 1826, the canal was kept open from late February through early December - its first full season. During that period, thousands of boats were entering the canal through the eastern terminus, and it was quite common for as many as fifty boats to set out in a single day. In the following years, traffic on the Erie became even heavier than that. As for the tolls collected that first year, they were almost too good to be believed. The Erie and Champlain canals took in $762,000 - about one-tenth the cost of building the two waterways, and five times the interest due on the outstanding bonds. Even the greatest optimists had expected nothing like this. By 1837, the Erie Canal Commission could report that the entire debt was repaid.

The bulk of the toll revenue came from freight. Before, it had cost about $100 a ton to transport goods by road from New York City to Buffalo. The average toll rate on the Erie Canal was a tenth of that. Rates were based on three factors: distance, weight, and type of freight. Leaflets were printed, with charts listing toll rates, and distributed to the canal boat captains. The highest tolls were charged for luxury items, such as silverware, china, and silk and velvet fabrics; boats that hauled brick, sand, clay, and manure paid the least. In 1826, more than 32,000 tons of manufactured goods (furniture, nails, iron, steel, and crockery), and more than 185,000 tons of agricultural products (wheat, flour, bacon, butter, cheese, corn, and potatoes) were transported on the canal.

Before 1830, the typical boat on the canal was flat-bottomed, seventy-seven feet long, and weighed nearly fifty tons with cargo. Because the locks were fifteen feet wide, the boats were restricted to a width of fourteen feet three inches. Most were towed by a pair of horses or mules. Later, the canal accommodated boats as long as ninety feet and weighing 100 tons including cargo. Within fifteen years, New York became the busiest port in America, moving tonnages greater than Boston, Baltimore, and New Orleans combined.

Besides the long-haul boats, a multitude of local craft cluttered the waterway. These boats had been built by men bitten by canal fever, and their creations were often strangely shaped and weirdly colored. The Erie also took care of a large amount of traffic from branch canals leading from Lake Ontario, and Seneca and Cayuga lakes. Rafts brought produce from hundreds of farms along these waterways to join eastbound shipping on the Erie Canal.

"In Our Adventurous Navigation"

The Erie had taken its place as one of the wonders of the world, and people flocked from all over to experience it. These included wealthy tourists from Europe, politicians, celebrities, and writers.

British stage actress Fanny Kemble, on a canal-boat tour of America in 1830, proclaimed New York's harbor "the most beautiful in the world," with its boats "glancing like graceful sea-birds, through their native element." Kemble liked "travelling by the canal boats very much," though she protested the "horrible hen-coop allotted to the female passengers." Another Englishwoman, society writer Frances Trollope was less ambivalent in her review. "I can hardly imagine any motive of convenience powerful enough to induce me again to imprison myself in a canal boat under ordinary circumstances," she wrote. English novelist Harriet Martineau, after her ride down the canal, reported: "I would never advise ladies to travel by canal, unless the boats are quite new and clean, or at least far better than any that I saw or heard of. On fine days it is pleasant enough sitting outside (except for having to duck under bridges every quarter of an hour) and in dark evenings the approach of the boat lights on the water is a pretty sight; but the horrors of night and wet days more than compensate for all the advantages these vehicles can boast."

To these tourists and American writers such as William Cullen Bryant, Edward Everett Hale, and Nathanial Hawthorne, the Erie Canal was an exciting – if not altogether pleasant – adventure. Hawthorne, the native New Englander, described his canal ride in 1835: "Behold us, then, fairly afloat, with three horses harnessed to our vessel, like the steeds of Neptune to a huge scallop-shell, in mythological pictures. Bound to a distant port, we had neither chart nor compass, nor cared about the wind, nor felt the heaving of a billow, nor dreaded shipwreck, however fierce the tempest, in our adventurous navigation of an interminable mud-puddle - for a mud-puddle it seemed, and as dark and turbid as if every kennel in the land paid contribution to it. With an imperceptible current, it holds its drowsy way through all the dismal swamps and unimpressive scenery that could be found between the great lakes and the sea-coast. Yet there is variety enough, both on the surface of the canal and along its banks, to amuse the traveller, if an overpowering tedium did not deaden his perceptions."

The average canal passenger was much less discriminating. Westbound traffic was dominated by numberless emigrants. Some of them spoke with New England twangs, and others in all the accents of Western Europe. But the talk was always the same: land prices in Illinois or Indiana or Ohio; and how many bushels of corn an acre of the fertile prairie land could grow.

There were many songs popular on the canal in those years; and one, though it deserves no fame for the quality of its verse, truly caught the spirit of the times:

> Then there's old Vermont; well, what do you think of that?
>
> To be sure the gals are handsome and the cattle very fat.
>
> But who among the mountains, amid the cloud and snow would stay,
>
> When he can buy a prairie in Michigan-eye-ay.
>
> Yea, yea, yea, in Michigan-eye-ay.
>
> Then there's the state of New York where some are very rich,
>
> Themselves and a few others have dug a mighty Ditch

To render it more easy for us to find the way,

And sail upon the waters to Michigan-eye-ay.

Yea, yea, yea, to Michigan-eye-ay.

Of all of the craft that traveled the Erie water, the packet boat was queen. More colorful than a flatboat carrying freight, packet boats were usually trimmed in red or green. They were also the fastest boats on the canal – pulled by three horses instead of the customary two – and the most luxurious. A packet used the best horses and changed them often, sometimes traveled day and night, and always had the right of way. All other craft had to move aside when a packet boat's steersman shouted out a passing warning to their crews. Since there was usually a towpath on only one side of the canal, the boat being passed would have to relax its towlines and move over toward the opposite bank. The packet would then pass over these lines and continue on her way.

Packet boats ranged in size, but the most common were between sixty and eighty feet. Most of the space was given to the cabin, which served as a lounge, dining room, and sleeping quarters. But there was also a kitchen, bar, and room in the bow and stern for the steersmen, who maneuvered the boat by pushing off the banks with long poles. A typical packet boat carried thirty to fifty passengers, and no freight, and fares were four cents a mile. To travel from Schenectady to Utica (eighty miles), for example, a passenger paid $3.50. Cheaper fares – two cents a mile - were offered by the less luxurious line boats.

During the day, packet travel often provided pleasure and excitement. There was much to watch as the boat glided past forested areas, small villages, and through growing cities. Passengers could recline on a bench on the roof of the cabin. Others sprawled out in the cabin to read – sometimes books provided by a small on-board library – or to play games, and socialize. When waiting at the locks or if traffic became tiresome, they could always jump ashore and go for a short walk on the towpath. One of the most common ways of getting back aboard a canal boat was to wait on one of the low bridges that crossed the canal and then drop onto the cabin as the boat passed beneath.

Those same bridges, however, made it impossible for a passenger to fall into complete dreamy relaxation as he rode. Although canal crews had initially built over 300 bridges, even more were being constructed as the country along the canal became settled. Since it was cheaper, the bridges were built low, but this also made them hazardous for travelers. As a boat moved along, the warning cry came at regular intervals from the steersman: "Low bridge! Everybody down!" Anyone who failed to bend or crouch down near the deck was knocked down or swept overboard, and often seriously injured. Nathaniel Hawthorne wrote about the calamity that befell a Virginia schoolmaster who did not heed the warning and was "saluted by the said bridge on his knowledge-box." The writer "heard the dull leaden sound of the contact, and fully expected to see the treasures of the poor man's cranium scattered about the deck." Luckily, he wrote, "there was no harm done, except a large bump on the head, and probably a corresponding dent in the bridge."

Passengers were fed three tremendous meals a day. A typical

menu included several kinds of meat, fowl, and fish, as well as potatoes, two or three kinds of bread, various vegetables and pickles, a choice of pies and cakes, and of course, coffee and tea. When fares were first established, they included meals. It took no time at all for the sharp-witted to discover that they could go aboard a packet as passengers just at mealtime, stuff themselves with a huge meal, and then step ashore a half hour or so later after paying a fare of only a few pennies. It was all perfectly legal, but the fares were changed after many of the canal boat captains complained. Even then, passengers paid only about a penny more a mile for the meal service.

For packets running around the clock, fresh teams of horses, stabled along the way in line barns, were changed regularly. The speed limit on the canal was four miles an hour, to prevent the wash of swift-moving boats from wearing away the banks. However, packet captains often sped up their teams to six or seven miles an hour to gain time. Of course, by speeding, the captain was breaking the law and was liable for a fine of $10, but he could earn a great deal more than that by making good time. He would merely jump ashore at the toll collector's office, throw down his $10, and keep going.

Some captains were indeed highhanded. Many stories were told – often, but not always, tall tales - about illegal races on the canal. As two packets came to a lock, one boat would try to pass, and the other would fight to stay in the lead. Then, as the stories went, tempers would run high, insults fly back and forth, and one crew would violate all the rules of fair play and cut the other's line. Life on the canal could be rough.

At night, when the cabin became the sleeping quarters, narrow bunks were put up along the walls, where they were stacked two- and sometimes three-high. The forward part of the cabin was the ladies' section, and on the more elegant boats, a curtain was drawn across at night to separate it from the men's section. Otherwise, the men remained on deck until the ladies turned in, before descending to their own bunks.

The British writer Charles Dickens made a trip on a packet and described the way the cabin was transformed into sleeping quarters when night fell: "Going below, I found suspended on either side of the cabin, three long tiers of hanging bookshelves, designed apparently for volumes of the small octavo size. Looking with great attention at these contrivances (wondering to find such literary preparations in such a place) I descried on each shelf a sort of microscopic sheet and blanket; then I began to dimly comprehend that the passengers were the library, and that they were to be arranged edgewise on these shelves, till morning."

Mayor Philip Hone of New York City was not reminded of anything as pleasant as a library; he remarked that the sleepers were "packed away like dead pigs in a Cincinnati pork warehouse." With so many travelers clamoring for places, the packets were usually crowded far beyond what they had been built to carry. One British tourist reported that "mattresses completely covered the floor, on which people lay as close as possible. The dinner table was covered with sleeping humanity, more thickly than Captain Davis ever strewed it with beefsteaks, and those who lay under the table thought themselves favored, inasmuch as they could not be trodden upon."

The bunks were simply frames with canvas tacked over them, attached to the wall on one side but supported on the outside by chains or leather straps from the ceiling. The supports sometimes gave way, causing passengers to tumble – often laughing - to the floor two or three at a time.

There was absolutely no privacy. A person had to edge into his narrow berth with everyone watching. Of course under such conditions, there was little undressing for bed; most people took off no more than shoes, and perhaps a coat. Once in his bunk, the would-be sleeper found it too narrow and too close to the one above to allow him to turn over during the night. The boots of crewmen clumping overhead on the cabin roof, the symphony of snores and squalling children, and the assorted sounds of the busy canalside made the night something to be painfully endured by all but the most rugged.

Some of the experiences of this kind of luxury travel were humorous - at least to a person looking back on them. Frederick Gerstaecker, a German traveler, wrote about his night on a packet: "I awoke with a dreadful feeling of suffocation; cold perspiration stood on my forehead and I could hardly draw my breath; there was a weight like lead on my stomach and chest. I attempted to cry out - in vain; I lay almost without consciousness. The weight remained immovable; above me was a noise like distant thunder. It was my companion of the upper story, who lay snoring over my head; and that the weight which pressed on my chest was caused by his body no longer remained a doubtful point. I endeavored to move the Colossus - impossible. I tried to push, to cry out - in vain. He lay like a rock on my chest and seemed to have no more feeling."

In his plight, Gerstaecker just managed to reach his cravat pin and jab sharply right where the weight was heaviest. There was a cry of "What's that? Murder! Help!" from above. Then the weight was momentarily lifted, and Gerstaecker slid out and stood on the floor. In the dim lamplight, he discovered that the worn canvas of the bunk above had ripped, plopping his neighbor down onto his chest. The pin thrust had caused the man to jerk upward, allowing Gerstaecker to escape. But now the canvas split even more, so that the unfortunate man was sitting on Gerstaecker's bunk below, with his head and feet still in his own bunk, crying, half-asleep, "Help! Murder!"

Still, most accounts of packet travel indicate that it was a more comfortable way to travel than roads: It was the fastest, and by far the smoothest.

But packets could carry only the hand luggage of passengers and so were not useful to emigrant families going west to settle. A family with livestock, household goods, and other possessions usually traveled on a line boat - a freight boat which allowed settlers to set up camp and cookstoves on deck. A line boat's deck was a busy place, with children swarming over and around the various piles of belongings, while smoke rose from an assortment of stoves as women prepared meals for their families.

There was little luxury on a line boat. Sleeping on stacks of possessions was probably as comfortable as the cramped, stuffy quarters of the packets. Being in the fresh air could be pleasant on a clear day, but in an all-day rain, it was miserable.

A line boat was considerably slower than a packet and often

ran only during daylight. These line boats were operated by companies, and the quality of the equipment and teams used on them depended on how much money they were making from the business. This meant that, with old horses frequently changed, the line boat could make little more than fifty to sixty miles on a good day. But a packet boat could cover about eighty miles in twenty-four hours.

The life of a line boat captain was not easy. He needed vigilance to beat out competitors for freight; he needed stamina, and he often needed a clever pair of fists to help him settle disputes with other captains. The boats were the only homes many captains knew. Their wives cooked and kept house in the tiny cabins. They hung out washing on lines on the deck which were set low to prevent disasters at low bridges. Children were raised on board, and even the tow horses were part of the family. When the horses were not working, they were brought on board and kept in stalls.

Timber rafts were a type of craft particularly detested by all other boatmen on the canal. Long and clumsy, they were drawn by oxen, which could go no faster than a mile and a half an hour. A timber raft could be several hundred feet long, and was made up of as many as ten sections of logs, called cribs, hitched together. The cribs had to be uncoupled at locks so they could pass through one at a time. Canal regulations stated that other boats could take their turn with the cribs going through a lock, but it did nothing to make the rafters more popular.

There were many other kinds of craft on the waterway. Shanty boats, moored where the canal was broadest, were little more than shacks on rafts, but to their owners, they were home. Entire families lived out their lives and died on the Erie. There were also floating shops of tinkers and menders, traveling sellers of potions and liniments, water-borne penny museums, and a hundred other enterprises drifting from village to village.

There was freight to be moved west and produce to be shipped east. There were small fortunes to be made, land to be bought and sold, and a whole new country to be settled. All of this was made possible by the Erie Canal.

But the great canal, of course, had its limitations. Between Albany and Schenectady, even the fast packet boats took a full day to negotiate the twenty-seven locks over just twenty-four miles. At this section, many passengers got off the boats to ride one of about thirty stagecoaches that made the roundtrip daily. The stagecoach fare was sixty-two cents (equal to about $7.50 today), or two-and-a-half cents a mile.

The weather also presented problems. In the spring, heavy rain often caused the canal to overrun its banks. During the winter months, the canal water sometimes froze solid. When it became impossible to navigate the Erie, travelers and haulers reverted to the old ways, over land by wagon or foot.

It was the job of the canal crews - or "canawlers," as they were called – to get the Erie running again. These crews were always hopping off the boats to make repairs, and occasionally building dams to hold back the water until the repairs to boat or canal could be completed. There wasn't much to do in winter but wait for the canal to thaw. Then, there was a mad rush to get the canal ready for the boats. Sections of the canal and towpath, distorted by snow and ice, had to be repaired or rebuilt to remove impediments to travel.

There seemed to be no obstacles that either time or ingenuity could not overcome.

The Canawlers

The canals created their own world and developed their own breed of men. As a matter of fact, they were not even called canals; everyone who worked or lived on them pronounced the word "canawls." Some scholars say that it was the Irish work crews who first started saying it that way, others that it was the Dutch in upper New York state who twisted the sound in that fashion. In any event, it was a canawl, whether it was Erie water or a stretch of channel in sun-bonnet-and-sycamore country out in Indiana.

It took a great many people to run a canal. In 1845, there were an estimated 4,000 boats on the Erie with 25,000 men, boys, and women working on them. Then there was a large force of lock tenders, towpath walkers to constantly patrol the canal and watch for the first signs of a leak or break, and repair and maintenance crews. There was a tremendous number of people who did not work directly on the canal but whose canal-side shops and services took care of those who traveled or worked on it. And finally, there was a very mixed assortment of those who were there because the canal offered such a rich field for their operations: gamblers, thieves, exhibitors of dancing bears, fortune-tellers, and the like. A canal was a busy and exciting place to be.

The crew of a canal boat, not counting the captain, numbered anywhere from two to six men. A company-owned packet running day and night might have two steersmen, a cook, probably a general deck hand, and a driver who was changed with his team every fifteen or twenty miles. On a small, owner-run boat, there would be only the driver and a steersman; the captain would change off with the steersman and take care of a great many other chores.

A canal boat was steered by a very large rudder, which the steersman moved with a long, heavy tiller. A steersman had to be skillful, because his vessel was clumsy and there were an amazing number of things it could run into - other boats, the sides of locks and the canal, and bridge abutments. His importance is shown by his wages, which averaged $20 a month with room and board - very good pay on the Erie Canal. By comparison, a captain's wages were $30 a month.

But being a steersman could be quite dangerous, especially on the boats called bullheads. The bullhead was a cantankerous vessel: Except for the bow and stern decks, there was little walking space around the outside of the boat. Nor was there deck space between the front and rear cabins. If a person was anywhere but fore or aft when passing under a low bridge, the only place to go was overboard. There was a ballad about a man who took a job on a bullhead boat and promptly got knocked overboard. It ended like this:

> So canawlers take my warning,
> Never steer a bullhead boat,
> Or they'll find you some fine morning
> In the E-RI-E afloat.
> Do all your fine navigating,

In the line barn full of hay,
And the low bridge you won't be hating,
And you'll live to judgment day.

The man, or boy, who drove the tow team was called a
hoggee, an old Scottish word for a laborer. He had two or
three horses or mules hitched tandem - one ahead of the
other - and generally rode on the rear horse. But walking or
riding, the job was no picnic. A hoggee usually worked two
six-hour shifts a day on the towpath, regardless of cold, rain,
or sleet. In his off hours, he had to feed and water his team,
rub them down, treat chafed places and sores from rubbing
collars, and repair harnesses. If there was any time left, he
curled up in his clothes and slept.

A hoggee's hours on the towpath also involved more than
just keeping the team pulling. On the busy canal, boats were
constantly passing and overtaking each other. A daydream-
ing hoggee could get towlines tangled so quickly that his
team might be dragged into the canal. When two boats
traveling in opposite directions had to pass each other, the
steersman of the outside boat moved to the far side of the
canal (or away from the towpath). The hoggee then had
to draw his horses to the outside of the towpath and stop
them. This allowed his line to go slack so that it lay on the
bottom of the towpath and the canal. And then the inside
boat, with its horses pulling and its line taut, would cross
over the other towline and both boats would continue on
their way.

In spite of all the skill and responsibility involved in a
driver's work, most of the hoggees were boys barely into
their teens. Boys were popular with captains because they

were cheaper ($12 a month for men drivers and $7 to $10 for a boy was the common wage), and they were easier to bully and cheat. Some captains deliberately mistreated their young drivers toward the end of the season to try to make the boys run away in desperation without collecting their season's wages.

Various missionary societies tried to help the boy hoggees - who needed all the help they could get. One missionary, Deacon Eaton, served for five years on the Erie and left a book about his experiences. He estimated that out of the total force of 25,000 people working on the canal in 1845, nearly 5,000 were young boy drivers, many of them orphans. He wrote about one captain who threw a sick boy out in a swamp, where he was found the next day lying on logs onto which he had dragged himself; the boy died less than two hours later.

The deacon wrote about another boy, who was so ill that he fell off his horse and knocked himself unconscious, badly gashing his head. The unfeeling captain had the boy dragged aside and made the other hoggee take over and drive on. Someone asked a nearby lock tender if he would help, but he replied, "No, I wish he was dead. He is the wickedest boy on the canal." So the lad lay senseless in the hot sun for several hours. At last, a man came along who took pity on the boy, carried him to his home, and called a doctor. Days passed before the lad recovered his senses. When he was well enough, he was asked if he really was the wickedest boy on the Erie Canal, as the lock tender had said. He answered that he supposed he must be because after five years of being treated like a slave and cheated out of his pay, he had learned to lie, steal, and get drunk. The story, according to Deacon Eaton, had a happy ending. The boy recovered, got a job with a good captain, and five years later was a captain himself.

Boys were often drawn to the canal from the family farms along its route. Though New York State's economy would remain primarily agricultural until well after the Civil War, with the emergence of the Erie Canal, many men and women were abandoning the farms to work in the factories, textile mills, and stores that cropped up. For the boys, a canal boat offered a way to earn and contribute, as well as a taste of adventure. By one estimate, children made up about a quarter of the canal work force by the 1830s. In addition to driving the horses and mules, they did the most menial jobs – from scrubbing decks to untangling tow lines.

In 1847, a fifteen-year-old farm boy from Ohio named James A. Garfield went to work for his cousin, Amos Letcher, who was captain of the canal boat *Evening Star*. Thirty-four years later, after Garfield was elected the twentieth President of the United States, the story of his six weeks on the canal would be told by author Horatio Alger, who was famous for his "rags-to-riches" narratives. In *From Canal Boy to President,* an illustrated biography written for juveniles, Alger relates that young Garfield had decided to leave the farm to make a living at sea. He was the youngest of five children supporting their mother; their father had died when James was two years old. After trying to get on the crew of a schooner and being rejected, Garfield settled for a canal boat. His cousin, Captain Letcher, agreed to pay him $8 a month to drive the mules.

Garfield's short stint on the canal illustrates how hazardous it could be for both boys and men. He had been at it less than a day when the *Evening Star* became entangled with a passing boat, and he and the two mules were yanked off the towpath into the canal water. Garfield "found himself struggling in the water side by side with the astonished mules," wrote Alger. "The situation was a ludicrous one, but it was also attended with some danger. Even if he did not drown, and the canal was probably deep enough for that, he stood in some danger of being kicked by the terrified mules. The boy, however, preserved his presence of mind, and managed, with help, to get out himself and to get his team out." Later, the captain asked, "What were you doing in the canal, Jim?" And the boy answered, "I was just taking my morning bath." It was the first of fourteen times that young Garfield fell or was dragged into the canal. The last such incident was nearly fatal.

Garfield had been promoted by his cousin to steersman. As Alger tells the story:

> It was midnight, and rainy, when he was called up to take his turn at the bow. . . . He tumbled out of bed in a hurry, but half awake, and, taking his stand on the narrow platform below the bow-deck, he began uncoiling a rope to steady the boat through a lock it was approaching. Finally it knotted, and caught in a narrow cleft on the edge of the deck. He gave it a strong pull, then another, till it gave way, sending him over the bow into the water.
>
> Down he went in the dark river, and, rising,

was bewildered amid the intense darkness. It seemed as if the boy's brief career was at its close. But he was saved by a miracle. Reaching out his hand in the darkness, it came into contact with the rope. Holding firmly to it as it tightened in his grasp, he used his strong arms to draw himself up hand over hand. His deliverance was due to a knot in the rope catching in a crevice, thus, as it tightened, sustaining him and enabling him to climb on deck. . . .

"God did it," thought James reverently. "He has saved my life against large odds, and He must have saved it for some purpose."

Shortly after, Garfield became ill, went home to recuperate, and was convinced by his mother to postpone his return to the canal for a year so he could attend school. He never went back.

Despite such harrowing tales, the Erie was easy navigating compared to many later canals - especially those that entered streams for portions of their courses. These added currents, sandbars, and other hazards to the ordinary problems of canal boat handling. Yet the best-known song about the terrors of shipwreck along the towpath is a ballad about "The E-RI-E." The first, third, and sixth verses give an idea of some of the fearful experiences that could beset a sailor on the canal:

We were forty miles from Albany,
Forget it I never shall;
What a terrible storm we had that night.

On the E-ri-e Canal.
O-o-oh, the E-ri-e was a-rising,
The gin was a-getting low,
And I scarcely think
We'll get a drink
Till we get to Buffalo-o-o,
Till we get to Buffalo.
Our captain he came up on deck
With his spyglass in his hand,
And the fog it was so tarnal thick
That he couldn't spy the land.
The winds began to whistle
And the waves began to roll,
And we had to reef our royals
On the raging canawl.

The perils of a raging storm on a channel four feet deep and forty feet wide were, of course, quite exaggerated. Even where the depth was seven feet and the width increased, the danger of shipwreck was slight. But many boats had accidents on the Erie - and on other canals throughout the country.

Another important member of the canal force was the tow-path walker, or pathmaster. His job was to patrol a ten-mile section of towpath and berm each day. The principal tool of his profession was a sack full of manure and hay. If he found a small leak, he stuffed the mixture inside it and sealed it by stamping it down. If the leak was beyond such simple repair measures, he called frantically for help. Muskrat burrows in the banks were a common cause of leaks, and the animals were thoroughly hated by canawlers. A small leak could grow so quickly that whole sections of bank would suddenly crumble away. Then the water would drain out of the canal leaving boats mudlarked on the bottom.

Slim and speedy repair boats pulled by fast horses were stationed at intervals along the canal, ready to answer emergency calls at a moment's notice. On board were ropes, shovels, timbers, hay, axes, and everything else needed to repair a breach. They foamed along at ten miles an hour, and were appropriately called "hurry-up boats." When there was a break in the canal, everyone - boat crews and lock tenders alike - worked night and day to get it repaired, because there was no way to detour around a section without any water in it.

For a lock tender, there wasn't much sleep to be had on the canal. There were times when boats would be waiting to go through the locks twenty-four hours a day. Although he had a few assistants, the lock tender had to be on hand most of the time himself to supervise the seemingly endless openings and closings of the lock gates.

"Full of Life and Activity"

Stops along the canal route offered some reprieve for the tired canawlers. Stretched out along the canal were the shops that catered to the canal boats. A captain could tie up in front of them and buy a firkin – a small cask - of salt mackerel or a bushel of oats, have a horse shod or get a gallon of whiskey, and pick up the latest news at the same time. There was a grocery store, and sometimes two, at every lock - and in those days, they sold much more than food. Almost all of them carried liquor which, being very cheap, was drunk in great quantities.

The Erie Canal itself affected the people and territory of western New York State like strong tonic. Before the Erie was dug, only the Mohawk Valley end of the route was populated, and some of that pretty thinly. From Rome west to Buffalo, there was only wilderness except for rare scattered clearings where a few cabins clustered together and pretended to be a village. But how they grew!

Colonel William L. Stone, who made a trip on the Erie in 1829, had been over the same course nine years earlier when the canal was being built. His remarks about Syracuse were typical of his amazement at the changes he found: "I looked about upon the village as I stept upon shore with still more astonishment than at Utica. 'Another enchanted city,' I exclaimed, as I glanced upwards and around upon splendid hotels and rows of massive buildings in all directions - crowded, too, with people all full of life and activity! Nine years before, I had passed a day here among some five or six scattered tenements . . . the whole being surrounded by a desolate, poverty-stricken, woody country, enough to make an owl weep to fly over it."

In truth, Syracuse was not so enchanting. It was still a new and raw community, and completely without trees. Colonel Stone observed that the people in all the new villages seemed to look on the forest as their enemy, and they cut down every single tree. But the colonel noted that after a year or two, the settler, detesting his ugly, treeless village, "now hates worse the clearings, and so all are busy planting saplings which will take a hundred years to equal their predecessors."

Syracuse was a city of salt. Springs of briny water came out of the earth, and even before the canal was built, salt was already being extracted from them. But the saltmakers had a hard time getting their product to market, and the industry remained small. Then Clinton's Ditch came, and Syracuse began to ship its salt everywhere - by the thousands of tons. Dozens of saltworks sprang up, and the city became the greatest salt producer in the nation.

Other canal communities also developed their own industries. Stump Town became so prosperous by shipping its fine buckskin gloves to market on the canal that the town changed its name to Gloversville. Amsterdam put in a rug loom and did so well that in time, it became a national center for carpet making. The residents of Little Falls switched from their old boat-hauling service to manufacturing. A gazetteer for 1840 listed the local industries as four iron furnaces, three paper mills, a woolen mill, two plaster factories, a machine shop, a fulling mill for cloth, a trip hammer, a brewery, a distillery, and a window-sash factory. It was the Mohawk River, rushing over the falls, that provided power for all this industry. But water power alone would not have brought in factories. Without the Erie Canal to transport its products, Little Falls would have remained no more than a village by a beautiful waterfall.

Rochester was a great boom town on the western half of the Erie. Here the canal crossed the deep and rugged Genesee River, which tumbled over rapids and waterfalls, ready to power new industry. The swiftness of Rochester's growth was fantastic. The clearing crews hurriedly felled trees to make more room for buildings, but had no time to pull stumps. So while the town boomed, the stumps left in the streets began to sprout. It was said that when the population reached 13,000, the streets were still so filled with brush that a stagecoach took an hour to thread its two-mile course through town.

But no one worried about a little brush in the streets with new industries springing up every day. The racing waters of the Genesee gave power to one waterwheel after another as the new factories started up. Stores began selling goods even before their roofs were finished. Speculators were buying up building lots in the uncleared forest and quickly selling them for huge profits. Eleven flour mills made Rochester one of the greatest milling centers in the world. Her mill-stones turned night and day, grinding out flour so endlessly that warehouse space ran out, and the barrels of flour had to be piled in the open. Rochester also became the center for canal boat construction. Hundreds of vessels were turned out in her boatyards; and by 1835, nearly half the boats on the Erie were owned or controlled by Rochester interests.

But with the rewards, the canal also brought ruin. Frequent drunkenness led to violence aboard the boats, which spilled over into the towns. Mobs of Irish canawlers rioted. Hapless youths, runaways, and orphans who worked summers on the canal boats formed gangs - such as the "Canal Boys," who terrorized Syracuse. For them, the canal became a school of corruption, "just the place," according to one study, "to put them through all the gradations of crime, from stealing a six-penny loaf or a bundle of hay up to . . . even murder itself." So flawed was the Erie Canal by im-morality that many began to refer to it as the "Big Ditch of

Iniquity." Believing the moral decline was a result of excessive drinking, New York canal commissioners tried in 1833 to prohibit liquor use by canal workers, but it was impossible to enforce. At least one company of canal boat owners announced that they would employ only "men who do not swear nor drink ardent spirits." Some of the more restrained canawlers joined to form the Erie Canal Temperance Society in 1835. Still, little changed.

Districts closest to the canal were filthy, crowded with shacks and shanties. The canal water itself reeked, having become a depository of both human and animal waste. These conditions and the heavy, almost constant flow of people combined to spread disease, which many believed was the punishment for the sins of the canawlers.

Of all the many events that touched the Erie communities, the most tragic was a devastating epidemic of cholera. The outbreak of the highly contagious disease started in Asia. Spread by infected travelers, it reached out across Europe and was then carried to Canada by three or four boatloads of Irish immigrants. The epidemic struck Montreal and Quebec in the spring of 1832. Within eleven days, it had killed more than 3,000 people. Before the summer was out, some 600 more lay dead in each Canadian city.

More travelers carried cholera along the St. Lawrence River and down the Champlain Canal to Albany, as well as from New York City up the Hudson. Albany had its first death in mid-June. From there, the disease raced down the Erie Canal carried by victims who probably felt fine when they started, but suddenly became sick - and often died - on the way.

Doctors at that time did not know what caused cholera. At first, they tried to comfort the general public by saying that the illness was not contagious and that its victims were almost always from the lowest level of society - the shiftless, the ignorant, the drunkards. Just shun strong drink, the medical men said, and close your windows tight at night to keep out the dangerous night air, and all would be well. But when the rich as well as the poor, and the hard-working as well as the shiftless, were struck down, the doctors had to admit that they could give no definite answers.

One fairly accurate theory held that cholera came from tainted soil and reached humans through fruits and vegetables they ate. But then the Utica newspaper quoted an unnamed authority who proposed that people wear wooden shoes so that they would not absorb the cholera influence through their feet. The most prevalent theory, however, was that the disease was spread by some sort of mysterious vapor in the air. According to one story, the citizens of Syracuse tested out the vapor theory by tying a large beef roast to a church steeple. When it was brought down an hour later, it was completely rotten, or so it was claimed. But many people suspected funny business and believed the meat must have been fairly rotten when it was put up. Some other canal towns, nevertheless, took to putting large pieces of meat on poles in the hope that it would soak up the cholera vapor in the air.

Nothing seemed to slow the spread of the disease. Few places along the canal were spared. Those who could fled the towns to high country. Hoping to avoid contact with the dreaded disease, farmers refused to transport produce to cities and towns. Stores closed and food became scarce.

Soon, people were actually dying in the streets. The air along the canal was murky from burning barrels of tar, which many communities kept going night and day in the belief that the heavy black smoke rid the air of cholera. Lime was believed to have the same power, and vats of it bubbled and fumed on street corners.

There were very few hospitals anywhere in 1832. Emergency hospitals were set up in an abandoned warehouse in Utica, a canalside barrel factory in Rochester, the poorhouse in Albany, and similar large buildings in other towns. The sick were so numerous that they crowded every inch of space. They were laid on beds of straw on the floor in suffocating, evil-smelling wards, where the windows were tightly closed against the night air with its supposed poisons.

Very soon, traffic on the canal had almost completely stopped. Some communities refused to allow boats to enter their borders. Others rushed the boats through, not even allowing passengers who had reached their destination to get off.

The epidemic was not limited to the Erie Canal. It quickly spread to Boston and other ports about the same time it hit Canada. It was carried west and south by infected passengers who changed from canal boats to ships on the Great Lakes. From there, cholera raced down the Mississippi River and its branches. It missed few places where men went: 10,000 people died in New Orleans that summer.

With the coming of autumn, however, the disease seemed to have run the course of susceptible people. Slowly, things began to return to normal. Captains waited impatiently at locks, wanting to make up at least some of the season's lost time before freeze-up. Hoggees shivered in the early morning chill as leaves dropped from the trees and rustled on the towpath. But the afternoon sun was still warm, and soon small boys fished once again from the berm, and housewives gossiped from their back porches. It seemed wiser to everyone to look toward the future rather than back on the months of terror.

5

THE CANAL CRAZE

Even before the Erie was completed, canals were being dug and plans drawn up for canals in half a dozen other states. Some were sensible, modest waterways, designed to help farmers get their produce to market, and to help miners and millers reach the seaboard with their products. But far too many canals were built on dreams, and they were often just about as solid.

The success of the Erie had made everyone canal-crazy. Those men who had said that the Erie would never pay for itself were now predicting success for every half-hatched plan to build a canal that came their way. The clink of money dropping into the toll collectors' boxes in New York interfered with good, straight thinking. No one stopped to consider that the Erie was prosperous because it lay in the only passage through the Appalachian wall. No other canal could possibly have such a clear advantage.

Actually, only a few canal systems were built to compete directly with the Erie for a share in the tremendous Western market. And only one of these actually made it across the mountains - the Pennsylvania system, or the Mainline as it was then called. It was the most complicated of them all: a weird combination of waterways, horse-drawn railways, and cable cars.

Philadelphia, like Boston and Baltimore, had not been over-joyed by the success of the Erie Canal. New York City had been outstripping them all in commerce and growth since 1807, and the Erie made New York even more prosperous. Philadelphia decided to build a canal which would bring lucrative trade back to the city and the state. So what if there was no break in Pennsylvania's western mountains, the city's leaders declared: Put the canal over them! With this spirit, the canal system became one of the engineering marvels of its day - but it was so complicated that it could never pay for itself.

Construction on the Pennsylvania system started with the usual hurrahs, fireworks, and spades full of earth on July 4, 1826. (Since the groundbreaking ceremony on the Erie on July 4, 1817, it had become almost an unwritten law that canal building should start on Independence Day.) From that day, the new canal went ahead full speed. Many of the engineers had worked on the Erie Canal, and they made good use of that experience. But they could not overcome the geographic fact that Pennsylvania was not a good place to build a canal to the West.

When the various parts of the canal's main route were finished in 1834, travelers got quite a ride for their money. The system, running on land and water and almost in the air from Philadelphia to Pittsburgh, became known as the Grand Canal.

Leaving from Philadelphia on the first leg of the journey, passengers traveled on a conveyance called the State Railroad, which consisted of coaches with railroad-car wheels that were pulled by horses to the foot of a long, high hill. The horses were unhitched, and the coaches were then drawn to the top by a powerful cable. At the summit, two or three coaches were coupled together, new horses hitched on, and they were off, on this oddest of canals, to Columbia, about seventy-five miles away. There, at last, the traveler boarded a boat. From Columbia, a true canal ran 173 miles beside the Susquehanna and Juniata rivers through 111 locks, as far as Hollidaysburg. At that town, the waterway ended, and an even more peculiar part of the trip began.

As the crow flies, Hollidaysburg is only thirty-five miles from Johnstown, but between the two lies the crest of the Allegheny Mountains. To reach one town from the other, one must travel up and down almost 2,600 feet. By comparison, the Erie had ups and downs totaling only 688 feet in 363 miles. A canal between the two points could only have been a huge series of locks, and it would have taken a couple of days to get a boat through. The engineers met the challenge by building another "railroad" over the mountains. This one, finished in 1828, was called the Portage Railroad, and it was another of the many canal-inspired engineering triumphs.

Passengers got into cars whose wheels rolled on wooden rails capped by iron bars; they were then pulled up the slopes by great ropes (later wire cables) drawn by engines above. There were five separate slopes, or inclined planes, carved in the mountain on either side of the summit, with level stretches of several miles between the top of each slope and the bottom of the next. After a car had been drawn up one inclined plane by motorized cable, horses pulled it to the bottom of the next. At the summit, there was a hotel, where travelers could spend the night before starting down the other side. All of this made for a great deal of hitching and unhitching. Even in its most efficient period, the Portage Railroad required thirty-three power changes.

The railroad ended at Johnstown, on the western side of the mountains. Passengers then boarded a canal packet once more for the trip to Pittsburgh, where the Grand Canal ended at the Ohio River. On the Ohio, steamboats and flatboats headed straight into the promised land. The trip from Philadelphia to Pittsburgh was 394 miles and required four full days. It included two railroads and two separate canal sections with 177 locks, almost twice as many as the Erie. The builders originally planned to extend the canal from Pittsburgh to Lake Erie, but they were so discouraged by mounting costs and the difficulties facing them in the remaining miles that they never pushed construction beyond Pittsburgh.

The Portage Railroad became something that all visitors to the United States wanted to see. Charles Dickens, who had been so amused by sleeping arrangements on an Erie Canal packet, was very impressed by his trip on the railroad. As he described it: "Occasionally the rails were laid on the extreme verge of a giddy precipice; and looking from the carriage window, the traveler gazes sheer down, without a stone or scrap of fence between, into the mountain depths below. . . . It was very pretty traveling thus at a rapid pace along the heights of the mountains in a keen wind, to look down into a valley full of light and softness, catching glimpses, through the trees, of scattered cabins . . . men in their shirt sleeves, looking on at their unfinished houses, planning out tomorrow's work, and we riding onward, high above them like a whirlwind."

The Grand Canal was completely opened in 1834, nine years after the Erie. Like New York State, Pennsylvania later went on to add branches to the canal system.

During the heyday of the Erie, connecting canals laced New York. A waterway was completed to Oswego on Lake

Ontario in 1828, finally accomplishing what the old Western Inland Lock Navigation Company had attempted in the 1790s. Cayuga Lake and Seneca Lake were tied to the Erie; the Genesee Valley Canal provided a link to the Allegheny River and thus to the Ohio; the Chenango Canal extended southwestward from Utica on the Erie as far as Binghamton; and the Chemung Canal, running south from Seneca Lake, linked up at the state border to a branch of the extensive Pennsylvania canal system. Most fantastic was the Black River Canal, connecting the Erie at Rome with the Black River to the north; it required 108 locks in only thirty-five miles. But by 1877, the state would begin disposing of some of these lateral canals, which by then had long since outlived their usefulness.

The handicap of having to transfer passengers and freight from one carrier to another was later partially overcome by building sectional canal boats. The sections, with freight and passengers aboard, were loaded onto railroad cars at Philadelphia and hauled to Columbia. There they were put in the canal and fastened together to form a canal boat for the trip to the Portage Railroad. At the railroad, the boat was uncoupled again, the sections hauled over the tracks, and coupled once more for the trip by water to Pittsburgh.

The Pennsylvania canal system with its specially built boats, its numerous locks, and its two railroads was both slow and expensive. It never paid its way and ran the state deeply into debt. Yet, contemporary accounts claim that during its peak, the system was so crowded day and night that at least forty boats carrying westbound freight and travelers could be counted at any place along the Grand Canal.

On July 4, 1828, President John Quincy Adams delivered his speech and thrust a spade into the earth on the banks of the Potomac River just above Washington. He struck a root, tried again, and hit another. Then he took off his coat, grasped the spade firmly, and on his third try, thrust it deep and turned over a good shovelful of earth, delighting the cheering crowd. The ceremony marked the first true challenge to the Erie Canal for a share in the commerce with the West.

This was a new beginning for the Potomac Company, first organized in 1785 to dig a similar canal. The company ran out of money before it could finish the proposed waterway, but it did manage to build twelve locks. Many of these were in good condition when the company was reorganized in 1825 to build the Chesapeake and Ohio Canal. It was to run beside the Potomac to Cumberland, Maryland, and then cross the mountains to the Youghiogheny River, a tributary of the Ohio, which offered a direct avenue to the West.

The city of Baltimore wanted to get in on the great project, and immediately made plans to dig a branch canal from the city to join the main waterway. But that idea was quickly dropped when a brief survey showed that the great number of locks needed to climb over the hills would make the branch far too costly. It was decided, instead, to build a railroad. So, on the same day President Adams was having so much trouble with the roots, another ceremony was being held in Baltimore to launch the first horse-drawn segment of the Baltimore and Ohio Railroad.

The C & O Canal progressed slowly. Sickness plagued the workers. The Irish and German immigrant work crews disliked each other so bitterly that they had to be kept apart to prevent fights. And even Irishmen from different counties in the old country engaged in monumental battles, helped along by plentiful supplies of cheap whiskey. Construction was often difficult, and at one point, a tunnel more than half a mile long had to be dug.

Legal troubles with the Baltimore and Ohio Railroad also slowed progress on the canal. When the railroad reached the Potomac, the company decided to keep on laying track, and continued to run alongside the canal. At one place, there was a narrow pass wide enough for only one of them. A long court battle ensued, but the canal emerged victorious. Not to be stopped, the railroad tunneled through the rock and again continued along beside the canal. By that time, the railroad had long since changed its horses for steam engines.

The Chesapeake and Ohio Canal got as far as Cumberland, Maryland, where it was to have started over the mountain crest - but there it stopped. The completed portion was 185 miles long and had cost over $11 million, far more than anyone had thought possible. And that was the end of one more dream, although the canal continued to carry freight, especially coal, long after many other waterways had fallen into disuse.

The canal frenzy even reached out to the new states on the western side of the mountains. Ohio, Indiana, and Illinois had all gained statehood by 1818, but seven years later, they were still sparsely settled and woefully underdeveloped. News of the Erie Canal struck a happy note on the frontier. At that time, road builders were not able to construct highways that could bear up under bad weather and heavy use, so rivers remained the only efficient means for hauling goods and passengers. The frontier states decided that the best way to bring settlers and commerce to the wilderness was to build their own canals as quickly as possible.

De Witt Clinton took time off from work on the Erie to break ground for a canal system in Ohio on July 4, 1825. The state had an extremely ambitious and complicated plan: It consisted of two main canals running generally north to south the length of the state, from Lake Erie to the Ohio River. Clinton broke ground first for the easternmost of the two, called the Ohio and Erie Canal. Then he journeyed clear across the state to launch the other waterway - the Miami and Erie Canal.

Work on the two canals continued for eight years. Sickness again was a greater obstacle than engineering problems, as clouds of malaria-carrying mosquitoes swarmed in swamps and bogs. It was believed then that whiskey helped ward off the combination of fever and chills, and every crew had a man who came around every few hours to hand out shots of the strong remedy to the diggers.

The Ohio canals soon found their own champion, a man named Alfred Kelley. Like Clinton, Kelley kept pushing construction year after year in spite of engineering problems, money shortages, sickness that laid his workers out, constant exposure to weather, and often personal danger. He grew so weary toward the end of construction that the state legislature ordered him to take a vacation, but he paid no attention to them. Finally, his weakened health forced him to conduct all business from bed. It appeared that only a miracle could keep him alive to see the completion of his canals - but years later, Alfred Kelley was still an active politician.

The Ohio canals were largely finished by 1832, although the Miami and Erie did not reach the lake until 1845. The Ohio and Erie Canal was 309 miles long and had 152 locks and fourteen aqueducts. The Miami and Erie Canal ran for 244 miles and had 105 locks and twenty-two aqueducts. Like most canals of the period, they never paid for themselves. But they did open up commerce for Ohio farms and villages, and enabled them to buy from and sell to the rest of the country. Thanks in great part to its hundreds of miles of commercial waterways, Ohio became the third most populous state in the Union before the canal era ended.

Cincinnati, Cleveland, Toledo, and Dayton all boomed from villages to great cities because of the prosperity the long-running Ohio canal system brought to them. Canals in other states also had their boom cities. But towns near waterways open only a short time often faded away again to tiny hamlets or a few moss-grown cellar holes.

Indiana was even less developed than Ohio. Except for the older settlements along the Ohio River, the state consisted of little more than a few handfuls of settlers trying to carve cornfields out of hardwood forests. The Hoosiers were bitten by the canal bug as early as their Ohio neighbors; but there were so few of them, and the job was so big, that all they could do for several years was discuss routes. Finally, in 1832, they decided to connect the upper Wabash River with Ohio's Miami and Erie Canal in order to reach Lake Erie.

This project was not spared the plague of disease either. It was said that over one stretch of canal, a worker died for every six feet of completed channel. Cemeteries were closed when they contained 1,000 bodies, and new ones were started. Recruiters were busy in the East luring new workers with offers of $2 and roast beef every day. This kept them coming, though too few lived long enough to enjoy many paydays.

When the first section of the canal was opened, the Hoosiers were so enthusiastic over their waterway in the wilderness that the legislature voted to extend it farther south along the Wabash. A year later, the representatives voted to add still more miles, with a big loop down to the central part of the state. Before it was all over, they had lengthened it once more, all the way to Evansville on the Ohio River. That made it 397 miles long - one of the longest canals built in America. The channel, however, did not reach the Ohio until 1851, and by then, railroads were beginning to steal away much of its business.

The Wabash and Erie Canal was open its entire length only a few years: It was a colossal financial failure. The tolls were never even enough to keep it in repair, and the state bore the crushing burden of a $17 million debt. But in another way, it was very successful: It brought people into Indiana and through Indiana to settle territories farther west. As a result, the Wabash and Erie Canal was even more important to the development of the West than the Ohio waterways.

Surprisingly, these backwoods canal men ran some of the fanciest packet boats in America. Some of the boats boasted furnishings imported from Europe, but Indiana boots, mud, and tobacco juice must have been hard on Brussels carpets.

The most famous of the Indiana packets was the *Silver Bell,* which was painted all in silver and was drawn by silver-gray mules whose harnesses sported silver rings and silver bells. Another packet, the *Indiana,* achieved some fame because she had a couple of Hoosier enthusiasts who were always on hand night or day to greet her in Fort Wayne. When they heard she was coming, they would drop whatever they were doing, rush to the canal, and play a concert on fiddle and clarinet. At the same time, it was typical of Indiana and the American West that very few boats provided either food or beds for passengers. Frontier hospitality took care of that problem. When the boat moored for the night, the passengers were expected to knock at a settler's door to obtain food and lodging.

The canal-building urge reached its westernmost limit with a waterway leading into the swampy village of Chicago. That canal, called the Illinois and Michigan, was built quite late, between 1836 and 1848. However, the fact that railroads, as well as the canal, were being constructed through the town caused a wild boom in real estate which sent prices up to fantastic levels.

Chicago's canal connected Lake Michigan with the Illinois River, which flows into the Mississippi. Only a slight height of land separates the two, and it was no great problem to build the canal as far as LaSalle on the Illinois. There the canal boats met river steamboats. This waterway was surprisingly successful from the start. It never did much business as a packet canal, carrying only occasional picnic parties and annual Sunday school outings; but it was a busy freight handler. In 1848, sugar and other articles reached Buffalo from New Orleans by way of the Illinois and Michigan Canal nearly two weeks before the first canal boat of the season reached Buffalo on the Erie.

Fifteen years after the Erie's opening, there were more than 4,000 miles of canal in the United States. Most of the waterways had been started by optimistic men, who were certain that the merry sound of coins being paid for tolls on the Erie would be echoed on their own canals. It seldom worked out that way. The states which were stricken with canal-building fever ended up with a total debt of some $60 million - a frightening amount for that time.

Still, canal fever kept running high in New York. Even before the canal was finished, the politicians became convinced that Erie revenue could be stretched to build any number of additional canals. Many rural representatives demanded branch canals for their constituents, and the legislature saw fit to approve several that were not only difficult but costly and impractical as well. The Black River Canal running north from Rome required 108 locks to carry it up and down a total of 1,081 feet in only thirty-five miles; it took nineteen years to build.

The canal era began with the Erie and lasted until mid-century. Some of the channels continued in use after that time. But none of them achieved even a faint shadow of the success of the Erie Canal. There was only one Big Ditch.

Yet, all the canals were part of an important period in the growth and settlement of the country, when the West lay empty. They were a way of moving men and goods to the frontier when the growing United States most needed to strengthen its commerce and develop the promise of her bountiful territory.

End of an Era

The heyday of the canals lasted no more than thirty years. The era spans no definite period of time but runs from the digging of the Erie Canal to the middle of the century, approximately 1820-1850. By the end of that time, hardly a shovel was being turned on new waterways. Many of the existing ones soon fell into neglect and were abandoned. If tombstones had later been placed beside the miles of empty ditches and rotting locks, their epitaphs would read: "Here lies a great canal, done to death by the steam locomotive."

Yet, it was a canal which brought the first locomotive to the United States. The Delaware and Hudson Canal, which ran more than 100 miles from Honesdale, Pennsylvania, to Rondout, New York, operated packets and freight boats like most waterways, but its main business was hauling anthracite coal. To get the coal from the mines to the canal at Honesdale, a sixteen-mile railway was built in 1826. The cars ran along an inclined plane and coasted to their destination. Not long afterward, the company learned that English mines had been successfully using steam locomotives on mine railways since 1811. So they decided to try steam themselves and sent an order to England for a locomotive. The shiny new Stourbridge Lion made only one run. The engine itself proved successful, but the roadbed on which the tracks were laid had not been built to sustain such a heavy load for repeated runs. Sadly, the company retired the Lion to a shed, and it never moved under its own power again.

Other locomotives, however, were soon in full-time operation. On Christmas Day in 1830, an American-made locomotive began running on a railway in Charleston, South Carolina. Unfortunately, it blew up six months later, fatally injuring the fireman who was sitting on the safety valve to stop the annoying hiss of escaping steam.

Peter Cooper, a wealthy manufacturer from New York, built his tiny locomotive, the Tom Thumb, for the Baltimore and Ohio Railroad. He set up a contest between his engine and a well-known racehorse to prove that steam could do better than horses. The Tom Thumb lost when a leak in the boiler lowered the pressure and seriously cut down its speed. But the test still managed to demonstrate the increased possibilities of steam. Before long, locomotives were replacing horses all along the Baltimore and Ohio Railroad.

About the same time, another railway company, the Mohawk and Hudson, went into competition with the Erie Canal. It ran seventeen miles from Albany to Schenectady and tried to win away those canal boat passengers who wanted to avoid the tedious journey through the many locks between the two towns. But the railroad gave its passengers a terrifying ride. They were seated on open flatcars which raced along at twenty miles an hour. They were choked and blinded by thick, sooty smoke, and constantly menaced by showers of fiery sparks. It was even doubtful that the train would be able to stop at the end of the trip, and track had to be laid up ramps to hold the train if the brakes failed.

At the time, this steam-powered joy ride offered little serious competition to the Erie. At first, the railroads were not permitted to haul freight except when the Erie was closed in winter, and even then they were forced to pay canal tolls on what they carried; but this restriction was removed in 1851, and the rail lines became full competitors. In later years, the Mohawk and Hudson became one of the links in the New York Central Railroad system which, in turn, became one of America's big freight and passenger carriers - and seriously cut into the Erie's business.

During the 1830s, other railroads appeared here and there, as far west as Michigan and Indiana. But the canals were still the darlings of the nation, as railways were only in the experimental stage. The men who were pinning their hopes on cars that ran on rails were not even sure how they were going to propel them. Some companies, like the early Baltimore and Ohio, depended on horses. Others experimented with putting the horse on a flatcar, where it walked on a treadmill geared to the wheels. Even sails were tried, and they worked fine as long as there was a wind - and it was blowing from the right direction. But it was the steam locomotive which eventually replaced all of these early methods.

Even while the canals were booming, the railroads were busy laying a few miles of track here, a few more miles there. The little locomotives were getting better, and they were less likely to break down or blow up. They were now able to haul more freight and passengers - even though they still had to stop every six miles to take on wood and water to fuel the engine. Very soon the railroads began to capture the public's attention. Many of the people who had clamored for the canals now considered them old-fashioned; they could be satisfied with nothing less than a railroad.

A great debate went on between those who wanted the

speed the railroads could provide, and those who supported the dependability of the canals. It was against God's law, said the canal people, for men to go roaring across the land at fifteen or even twenty miles an hour. Some doctors doubted that the human body could stand such speeds without suffering serious mental and physical ailments, including possible boiling of the blood. The railroad supporters pooh-poohed all of these arguments except the last. But most Americans, because of the great size of their country, were always in a hurry to get places, and rather liked the idea of all that speed.

As the years passed, a strange thing happened. People not only lost interest in the waterways with the coming of the railroads, but many of them developed an actual hate for the canals they had once welcomed with fireworks and cheers. By the middle of the century, men were gathering in protest meetings which often ended in raiding parties. They damaged locks, burned aqueducts, and cut holes into canal banks to let the escaping water rip out whole sections of channel.

It is difficult to understand such malicious destruction, especially when hundreds of thousands of people still depended on the canals for their livelihood. Part of it was due to the huge canal debt. Those same people who had pushed for the digging of so many canals now began to lay the blame for the debt on the waterways, instead of on themselves. The anti-canal fervor was also partly the result of ignorance and superstition. The idea had spread that the canals and their reservoirs carried agues and fevers.

Indiana's great Wabash and Erie Canal, which had cost so

much in human life and heartache and money - and yet had repaid everything by bringing the state out of the wilderness - was one of many victims of this senseless vandalism. In 1855, when the last mile of the long waterway was not yet quite done, a mob of men with disguised faces descended on the canal. They set an aqueduct afire and blew up the dam of the great Birch Creek Reservoir, destroying the water supply for a long section of canal. It was repaired at great expense after several months' work, but boats had hardly begun to move in the channel before the reservoir was wrecked again. It was repaired once more, and the people to whom the canal still meant a great deal rejoiced. But by then, the canal era was ending. Within four short years, flood damage, rotting aqueducts, and general neglect put sections of the Indiana canals permanently out of service more effectively than any of the canal-hating mobs had been able to do.

As sections of the canal fell into disrepair, they were abandoned, because people were convinced that expenditures for repairs were hardly worth making. Few, if any, of the man-made waterways had been able to recoup their building costs, or to set aside reserve funds for even emergency repairs in case of severe damage from floods or other unforeseen disasters.

In a few scattered areas, some sections continued to operate for years after the canal as a whole had ceased to carry traffic. Mule teams leisurely towed weather-beaten old boats down the remaining lengths of channel - passing through moss-grown locks to serve villages still far from any railroad. Finally, even these bits of canal went away.

The Pennsylvania Grand Canal, with its Portage Railroad and other expensive complications, did not last long after the canal era began to fade. But portions of the Pennsylvania branch canals saw mules and horses on their towpaths until well after the First World War. It was no longer an exciting waterway crammed with packets and line boats moving night and day. There were just a few ancient barges with crotchety old captains, hauling cargoes no more romantic than a load of coal. Nevertheless, they were canal boats, and they were among the last. Once these battered old barges ceased running along the canal, no new boats would come along to replace them.

The Chesapeake and Ohio Canal along the Potomac never got across the mountains as its backers planned, and it never made much money, but it had a longer life than most. More than once, it was badly damaged by floods and looked as though it would have to be abandoned. But each time, its backers managed to make the needed repairs. Finally, though, a flood in 1924 washed out great parts of it, and there was just not enough business to make more repairs worthwhile.

A small section of the Chesapeake and Ohio, however, is still operating; it is one of the last towpath canals in the country. The United States Government acquired the weed-grown waterway, repaired a part of it near Washington, and put a canal boat on it. Today, anyone who goes to the nation's capital can ride on a canal boat pulled by a team of mules treading a towpath in Georgetown.

Even though the hoggee and his team have long since made their last trip, and the towpaths themselves have disappeared, a few canals are still in use - with their faces greatly changed. Any boats that run along them now are pushed by tugboats, not pulled on towlines. But these canals are a pitifully small patch on the thousands of miles of waterway that once bustled with activity.

And what of the champion of them all? The great Erie Canal continued to make money while all the others were going into debt; it was always able to repair flood damage and the wear and tear of hard use. For a very long time, the railroads could offer no serious competition because the Erie still lay in the most convenient passage through the mountains. In the early part of 1825, half a year before it was completely opened, the canal commissioners reported that the Erie was already too small. They suggested that the locks be doubled, and even hinted that a parallel canal should be built in the eastern section to handle bigger boats and more traffic.

The work crews got busy in 1836. In some places, two sets of locks were built - all extended from ninety to 118 feet – so that two lanes of boats could pass through. The channel, which had generally been forty feet wide and four feet deep, was made seventy feet by seven feet. Many sections of the channel were straightened and relocated, reducing the Albany-Buffalo distance by thirteen miles. Many of the locks were made higher, eliminating several of the original eighty-three.

The enlargement program moved by fits and starts, tied to canal revenues, and was not finally completed until 1862, when heavy wartime shipping brought large toll collections. By then, the canal era was well past, and many waterways in other states had already returned to wilderness. But the Erie showed no sign of fading. After its enlargement, it could carry boats of up to 250 tons, yet it was still too small. In 1868, the canal carried more than 3 million tons of freight. During this period, and even into the 1880s, it was said that a person standing on a bridge could often see two long lines of boats in either direction as far as his eye could reach, and at night the string of headlamps looked like a torchlight parade.

By 1860, the railroads had grown so strong that they held tremendous political power in New York State and lobbied to stop canal operations. Some railroads campaigned for the draining of the Erie so that railroad tracks could be laid on its bed. But the Erie belonged to the people of the state, and its friends were able to ward off attacks on it. The packet boats had long since disappeared because they could not possibly compete with the faster passenger trains. But for carrying heavy freight in cases where speed was of no importance, the Erie had broader shoulders than the railroad.

In 1882, all tolls were abolished. By that time, the Erie had paid its original cost many times over. Even De Witt Clinton, for all his faith in the Ditch, could never have imagined that its tolls would clear $42 million. But after the turn of the century, towpath power came to an end for the Erie, too, although the waterway itself still continues a highly useful life.

Beginning in 1903, the Erie Canal and its two main branches - the Champlain Canal, and the Oswego Canal, which connected the Erie with Lake Ontario - were cut deeper and widened, and much larger locks with higher lifts were installed. This chain of waterways, completed in 1918, is known as the New York State Barge Canal System. Including the stretch along the Hudson River, the Barge Canal runs some 800 miles. Much of the old Erie Canal was relocated. It has boldly tamed the once-turbulent Mohawk River with a series of dams, turning it into just another placid length of canal. Huge barges, almost 300 feet long and pushed by diesel-powered boats, now move on a waterway where packet boats once paid fines for speeding faster than four miles an hour.

In some spots, the enlarged Erie and the old Erie still use the same course; but on most of the new route, one or both of the later canals have been shifted anywhere from a few feet to a number of miles from the former course. One can still find traces of the overgrown channels and sometimes even a lock - often within easy hearing distance of the whistle of a tugboat pushing barges of gasoline, steel beams, or grain on the modern canal.

Though the Barge Canal is still a workaday route, the color of the early years is no longer there. The canal-side grocery stores have gone, and there is no sound of a fiddle coming from a lock-tender's shack on a rainy night; those things went out with the old Erie.

The canal has often left a stamp even where it has disappeared. Erie Boulevards in Syracuse, Schenectady, Utica, Rome, and possibly other New York communities were not named accidentally; they were the routes the old Erie followed through those towns. But other historic spots have disappeared without trace; Lock Number One at Albany, which separated the early Erie canals from the Hudson River, is now somewhere under a truck parking lot.

Some abandoned segments of the Erie canals, being state property, were put to other state uses — as the right of way of a highway, for example. But well over half the total still lie empty and unused, silent reminders of the past.

One must imagine them as they were when the hoggee drove his team down the towpath, and the steersman shouted, "Low bridge, everybody down!"